Just Double the Recipe

JUST DOUBLE THE RECIPE

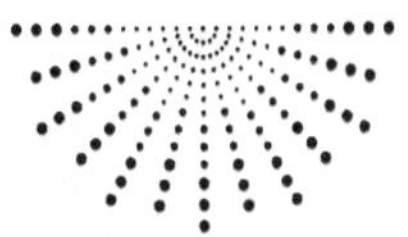

HEIDI RENEE MASON

If you love *Just Double the Recipe*, you might enjoy the other sweet and heartwarming love stories I have published:

LOVE AT FIRST CREPE

JUST DOUBLE THE RECIPE

ALWAYS HOPE

For information, contact the publisher, Hot Tree Publishing.

www.hottreepublishing.com

Editing: Hot Tree Editing

Cover Designer: Claire Smith

Formatting: Justine Littleton

ISBN: **978-1-925853-16-2**

This book is dedicated to all women everywhere. You are stronger than you know. It is also dedicated to my family, because no matter what I do, and no matter what I accomplish, you will always be my reason.

CHAPTER ONE

"Babe, your alarm has been going off for five minutes. Are you planning on getting up today?" Tate gently shook me awake.

"I don't want to get up yet. It's still dark outside," I groaned as I rubbed sleep from my eyes and then buried myself beneath the covers. To further demonstrate my distaste, I placed my pillow over my head.

"It's dark outside every morning at this time. You have to go to work. Your customers are hungry for crêpes." Tate rubbed my shoulders as he chuckled softly at my whining. "You're going to cause a riot in downtown Portland if you don't show up and cook for your fans."

"I obviously did not choose my career path correctly. Why does five o'clock in the morning have to get here so soon? I'd like it a whole lot better if it happened later in the afternoon." I moaned again, pulled my head out from under the pillow, and reluctantly rolled out of bed.

Early mornings and alarm clocks were not my friends. If I had my preference, I would like to awaken naturally, around noon. One would think I would be used to the early morning routine after having done it for so many years. One would be sadly mistaken. Even though my occupation as a baker demanded it, the sad truth was that I would never be a morning person. It just wasn't in my DNA.

Omelet, my finicky, opinionated gray cat, was curled up in a ball at the bottom of the bed. Normally she slept on my chest, or sometimes on my face. Boundaries and personal space were nonexistent with her. She was the equivalent of a temperamental toddler most of the time, but I loved her more than life itself. Omelet was a spoiled princess, and she knew it. She ruled the roost in my house.

She glared angrily at me, my movement disrupting her slumber. She sighed loudly, kneaded the space below her once again, turned her back to me, and covered her face with her paws. If cats were able to roll their eyes, I knew she would have been doing it. She hated mornings even more than I did, and she did not want to be disturbed before she was ready. Omelet was the best pet a girl could ask for, but she certainly knew how to hold a grudge. I would be working for days to get back on her good side after waking her up too soon.

"Babe, I'll be at work all night, so I won't see you until tomorrow." Tate grabbed my hand and pulled me close to him. "I didn't want to leave without saying goodbye."

He winked at me with those gorgeous green eyes of his as he pulled me tightly into a bear hug. His hugs were at the top of my list of favorite things. Being wrapped up next to my favorite fireman gave me the same sensation as sinking into a warm bubble bath, or taking the first sip of my morning coffee. It was pure perfection, and I couldn't seem to get enough of it. I couldn't believe it had taken me so long to decide that I wanted to be with him, but commitment had never been my thing. I was still trying to figure it all out.

"Don't remind me about your insane work schedule. Or mine either, for that matter." I sighed as I ran my fingers through his thick blond hair. "It's all right, though. Omelet and I will just stay in and watch some Netflix. There's a new documentary about how cats can read minds, not that I need convincing. I already know it's true. Besides, Marcus said he might stop by after I get off work."

"Marcus? What does he want?" Tate's jaw clenched, and I felt his body stiffen. He hugged me a little tighter. "Doesn't he have a wife to go home to these days?"

"You know very well that he has a wife. You and I both attended the wedding of the century, remember? Certainly you haven't forgotten. I was Marcus's best woman, and I looked adorable in my tuxedo-inspired gown." I chuckled and rolled my eyes, thinking of the ostentatious wedding Cinnamon's parents had organized when the happy couple was married last month.

The event was completely over-the-top, sort of like a three-ring circus minus the lions, tigers, and bears. It was the exact opposite of the kind of wedding I would have if Tate ever managed to get me down the aisle. The jury was still out on whether or not that would happen, although he was trying very hard. The word "wife" brought to mind the string of disastrous marriages my father had when I was growing up. Each one had been worse than the last. His third and current wife, Elizabeth, was definitely not my favorite person in the world, although the two of us had reached a mutual agreement to go easy on one another for Dad's sake.

Marriage to Tate signified change, and I hated trying new things. I was perfectly happy just the way things were. Besides, we had only been "officially" dating for about nine months, and engaged for one. He was ready to marry me within the next five minutes, but I thought it was too soon to even consider something so drastic.

"So... Marcus... why isn't he at home, watching Netflix with his wife?" Tate tried his best to make the question sound casual, but he wasn't fooling me. The idea of me hanging out with Marcus put him on edge.

"Cinnamon and my lovely stepmother are away on their annual 'best friends forever girls only' shopping trip to London. They've probably spent at least a million dollars by now. They'll be gone all week, so he's lonely. You won't be here anyway, so it's no big deal, right?" I pulled away and looked questioningly at my fiancé.

"Right... no big deal. I suppose not. Doesn't he have someone else he can hang out with, though? Why does it always have to be you?" Tate's handsome face twisted into a scowl.

"Because he's one of my closest friends, that's why. You're not still jealous of him, are you?" I put my hands on my hips and forced Tate to look at me.

"Jealous? Me? Why would I possibly be jealous of a guy who you admitted you were attracted to just a few months ago? Don't be silly." The sarcasm practically dripped from his voice.

Tate walked across the room and dug through his work bag. He pretended to look for something inside, but I knew it was just a ploy to avoid my penetrating glare. Any time the subject of Marcus Tucker came up, Tate all but shut down. I couldn't really blame him. After all, I admitted to Tate before we were a couple that Marcus and I had experienced an insane attraction toward one another. We discovered quickly enough that it was nothing more than physical, though. Our hearts belonged to other people. But although

Marcus and I had moved on, Tate couldn't quite push past it.

"Why are you still so prickly about Marcus? He's married to Cinnamon, and I'm engaged to you. We are nothing more than friends. When are you going to get that through your thick skull?" I couldn't believe we were still having the same old conversation. As much as I understood his feelings, they also irritated me.

"Willow, I am not threatened by Marcus Tucker. I just don't know why you can't hang out with a friend who's a little more... I don't know... female." Tate stuffed some boxer shorts into the duffel bag and zipped it shut.

"Have you met me? You of all people should know that I don't get along very well with other women. Why is this suddenly so surprising to you? You've been my best friend since we were six years old, and you're a guy. Other than Suzanne, how many women have you ever known me to be friends with?" I shrugged and shook my head. It was all so obvious. I didn't know why Tate couldn't see it.

"Think about it, Willow. We're best friends who fell in love and are now engaged. Forgive me for not being a fan of you spending so much free time with your other male friend, the super cop." Pain flashed across Tate's face, and my heart melted a little bit. It wasn't just jealousy. He really was still afraid of losing me to Marcus.

I walked across the room, wrapped both of my arms around his neck, pulled his face down to mine, and pressed my lips to his. I channeled all the love I felt for him in this kiss. His familiar taste of lemons and peppermint caused my stomach to flip. I rubbed my hands up and down his arms, taking the kiss even deeper, wanting to keep the connection between us for as long as we could. I wished we could just stay inside my room all day instead of being productive adults.

All too soon, our lips parted, and I placed my hands on each side of Tate's face and forced him to look at me. "Tate Randall, you have nothing to worry about. I love you, and only you. I've agreed to be your wife. Marcus is married to Cinnamon, and the two of us are just friends. My future is with you."

"Here's the thing. My heart knows all that, but my head gets in the way. I'm sorry." Tate shook his head slowly. "Something about that guy just sets my teeth on edge. But I trust you. I do. I love you, babe." Tate hugged me quickly and grabbed his bag. "Now I have to run or I'm going to be late. I'll call you later on. Have a good day at work."

"Love you too," I called to him as I heard the front door shut.

Omelet yawned widely, stretched, and leaped off the bed. Apparently, she was ready to begin her day. I leaned down to pet her as she rubbed her furry body on my legs. "Morning, baby. Sorry about waking you up earlier. I'll be more careful next time. Are you hungry?"

She meowed in response and trotted into the kitchen. She knew the drill.

I poured her favorite food into a bowl and mixed in some tuna. "I have so much to do today, Omelet. I'm completely swamped at work. As much as I don't want to do it, I know the time has come. I need to hire a new employee. If I'm going to buy that delivery bike, someone's going to have to ride it, and we both know it shouldn't be me. The last time I tried to ride a bike, I crashed into a tree and fractured my collarbone."

Omelet stopped eating and shook her head at me. She knew very well that I was a world-class klutz.

"How am I going to find someone I can trust?" I gave her a scratch behind the ear, and she cocked her head to the side skeptically. "Don't judge me, Omelet. Obviously it's something I need to work on. Trust doesn't come easily to me, as you well know."

I glanced away from Omelet's all-seeing eyes. She wasn't very sympathetic. Personally, I thought she should be more understanding of my shortcomings. I was working hard at becoming a better person, but something like that didn't happen overnight.

I decided to change the subject. "You're okay with staying home today, right? I think it's best for me to focus on interviewing potential new employees. I can do that better if you're not there to distract me." She smiled at me in agreement and finished the remainder of her breakfast as I ran to the bathroom to take a shower.

You'd better get a move on, Willow. It's time to stop complaining and be a grown-up.

CHAPTER TWO

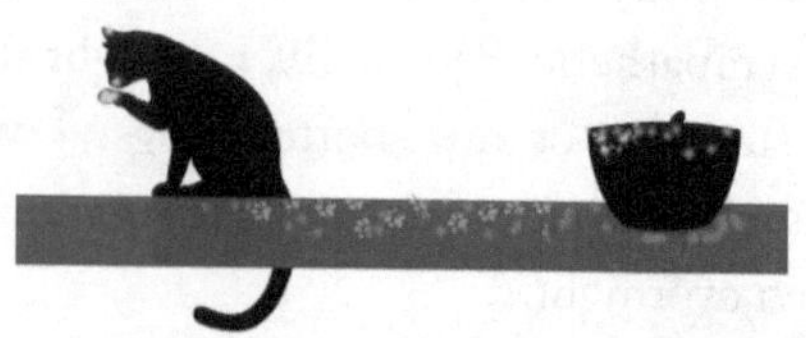

Thirty minutes later, I was ready to pretend that I was proficient at adulting. I'd thrown on my green polka dot peasant dress with my favorite yellow crocheted sweater. I hadn't done much with my still-wet red curls. Slipping my feet into my Birkenstocks, I situated my floppy flowered hat on my head, blew a kiss to Omelet, and headed out into the dark streets of Portland, Oregon.

The foggy, chilly June morning greeted me like an old friend. I soaked in the coolness, already dreading the warmer temperatures that would come once summer was in full swing. The sun and I did not get along, so I went into a sort of hibernation during the warm months, avoiding the ultraviolet rays as much as possible. Other than going to work, I basically became a hermit.

I had yet to discover what other people liked about summer. It was hot, sticky, and generally gross in my opinion. It didn't help that I broke out in a rash if the sun touched my skin. I might have enjoyed it more if not for that fun little fact. That's why I reveled in these dark, chilly mornings.

I ducked into the Simpson Coffee near my apartment and spotted my friend and favorite barista, Suzanne. Normally her hair was a dark green hue, but that morning it was a lovely shade of electric blue, and it suited her perfectly. Her eyebrow was pierced, and she had too many earrings to count. Her kilt and combat boots only added to her "I'm so much cooler than you are" vibe.

"Morning, Willow," she greeted me.

"Morning, Suzanne. I need a caffeine infusion, stat. Please make it strong," I requested as I dropped my bag on top of my favorite table and sat down.

"One butterscotch latte with extra butterscotch and an extra shot coming right up." She smiled in response, already hard at work on my drink. "Where's my little buddy, Omelet?"

"She's at home. I have a full day ahead of me, so I thought she should just stay put. Besides, she can be way too opinionated sometimes, and I don't need her judgmental ways today." I sighed heavily, wishing I could delay the inevitable task of hiring an employee.

I'd never had anyone work for me before, and I couldn't imagine myself as someone else's boss. I was barely responsible enough to handle myself. The thought of interviews and meeting new people made me want to run for the hills. Unfortunately, since I was the boss, I couldn't do that. I was going to have to suck it up and be an adult.

"I hope everything's okay at the Dancing Crêpe." Suzanne handed me the latte and casually leaned against my table to chat.

"Yeah, things are great. That's the problem, actually. Business has doubled in the last couple of months, and I can't keep up by myself anymore. I'm also hoping to buy a delivery bike, and that means I need to hire an employee." I took a sip of the butterscotch latte and closed my eyes in appreciation as the hot, sweet liquid slid down my throat.

"You won't have any trouble finding an employee. The Dancing Crêpe is one of the hottest food spots in town. You'll probably have people knocking down your door wanting to work there," Suzanne encouraged.

"For real? Do you think so?" I couldn't believe what I was hearing. *My food truck is considered a Portland food hotspot?*

"Yeah, I know so. I hear people talking about it all the time. How do you plan to advertise for the position?"

"I thought I would just put a sign in the window today and see what happens. Or better yet, maybe you want a job? You're my friend. You should come and learn to make crêpes." I wasn't trying to steal Dad's employee, but if I could get Suzanne to work for me, I was going to jump on it.

"I love you, Willow, but I've worked for your dad for years. He provides insurance and tuition reimbursement. Can you compete with that?" The twinkle in Suzanne's eyes told me that she knew my compensation package couldn't even come close to Dad's.

"No, you know I can't. But I had to try." I took another sip of my drink. "I'm really dreading the thought of someone working for me."

"That's because you don't trust people, and you're a control freak." Suzanne shrugged and returned to her spot behind the counter. "Of course, I mean that in the nicest way."

I giggled at her because she was right. She knew me pretty well. "If you weren't my friend, I might be offended by that."

"If you weren't my friend, I never would have said it to

you." She busied herself by wiping off the counter and the espresso machine.

"Do you have any advice for me? What kind of person should I hire? I need help." I was hoping Suzanne might be able to tell me what to do. I certainly had no idea.

"My advice to you is to hire a guy who is a creative, artistic type. Whoever you hire is going to be stuck in a small space with you day after day, and if it's another woman, you might just kill her. You know as well as I do that you don't get along with many women. Stick to what you know. You'll be more compatible with a man. That's just my two cents' worth," she offered.

"You're probably right. I do get along better with men. I was just trying to explain that to Tate this morning, as a matter of fact. He thinks I should branch out a little and find more female friends. You're pretty much my only one." I grabbed my latte, threw my purse over my shoulder, and stood to leave.

"You and I get along because we're the same. Generally speaking, we don't like the drama of other women, and we both understand that. Tate is only worried because he loves you so much, and he doesn't want to lose you to another one of your guy friends. Cut him some slack." Suzanne winked at me.

"Why does it all have to be so complicated? Adulting is hard." I rolled my eyes at her, waved goodbye, and stepped back outside.

I hopped on the MAX and got off at the stop nearest the Dancing Crêpe. Glancing at my phone, I saw I still had an hour before opening time. I unlocked the door of my food truck, flipped on the lights, and began my regimented opening routine.

I wiped down the counters before mixing up the batter

for the next day's crêpes, turned on the griddle, and made an inventory list. It was a big day. Not only was I starting the hunt for a new employee, but I was debuting a new crêpe on my menu. I hoped it would be a hit.

My newest creation, the Hunka Hunka Burnin' Love, was close to my heart. I'd worked hard to get it just right, and I'd finally figured out the perfect recipe. I had named it in honor of Tate, my fireman. It was my own sweet version of a crêpe Suzette, and as such, was flambéed. It seemed to me that a crêpe named after a fireman deserved to be set on fire.

Taking a deep breath, I grabbed a piece of poster board and wrote Help Wanted in curly, fancy lettering with brightly colored markers. I drew a couple of hearts and flowers on the sides to dress it up a bit, then taped it into the window of the food truck.

Flipping on the flashing Open sign, I told myself that I was ready to handle whatever came my way. I'd come this far by sheer will and perseverance, and nothing, not even the prospect of hiring a new employee, was going to stop me now.

CHAPTER THREE

"Do you want popcorn?" I presented the question to Marcus, who was lounging on my couch with his bare feet on my coffee table.

"Popcorn is fine, but do you have anything else? I'm really hungry. I didn't eat dinner tonight." He grinned at me, his chocolate-brown eyes twinkling mischievously.

"Of course you didn't eat dinner, because you knew you could come over here and I would feed you, like always." I rolled my eyes at him and rummaged through the refrigerator. Grabbing some smoked gouda, I put a pot of water on the stove to boil. "I'll make smoked gouda mac and cheese. How does that sound?"

"With pancetta crumbled on top like you usually do? Pretty please?" Marcus begged and batted his mile-long eyelashes at me.

"You know that's how I always make it for you, so don't whine," I scolded.

"You're the best, Willow." Marcus jumped up from the couch and joined me in the kitchen, where he planted a quick, friendly kiss on the top of my head. "How can I help you?"

"By getting out of my kitchen. You know I don't like to be bothered when I cook." I patted him playfully on the cheek and steered him back toward the living room.

"Fine, I'll go sit down like a good boy," he replied as he flopped back on the couch. "How was work today?"

"Busy, which is a great thing, I suppose. Did I tell you that I put a Help Wanted sign in the window today?"

"No, you didn't. That's a big step for you. How do you feel about being someone else's boss?" Marcus flipped through the channels on the television as he spoke.

"I feel just peachy about it."

"Hmmm, I'm sensing some of the usual Willow sarcasm that I know and love. What do you have against hiring an employee, anyway?"

"Seriously? Can you honestly picture me as anyone's boss?" I turned away from the stove and glared at Marcus.

"Well now, let me ponder that for a second." Marcus tilted his head to the side and pretended to think. "Nope, come to think of it, I've never had a boss who was as cute as you." He grinned widely.

"Shut up." I stuck my tongue out at him.

"Personally, I think you'd make a pretty cool boss. You're laid-back, you're open-minded, and you're fair. If I ever decided not to be a cop, I would come work for you in a second. Plus, like I said a minute ago, you're way easy on the eyes."

"What would your wife think if she heard you say that?" I smirked at him, knowing very well what she would think.

"She wouldn't be surprised at all. Cinnamon knows I

think you're a little hottie, and she's fine with it," Marcus chuckled.

"Somehow I don't believe that's true. She would rip my hair from my head if she heard those words come out of your mouth. It's a good thing she's thousands of miles away in London right now." I giggled, thinking of how jealous my long-time enemy would be to hear her husband call me a "hottie." Like Tate, Cinnamon wasn't a huge fan of the fact that Marcus and I were such good friends.

"You're probably right. Although to be fair, she hated you long before you and I ever knew each other," he reasoned.

"That's true. Her hatred of me goes all the way back to elementary school. Although, I do have to say that we've reached an unspoken agreement since the two of you got together. We try to keep our feelings buried a bit for your sake." I turned off the stove and drained the pasta.

"I appreciate it. Although, that was one of the conditions when we got married. She had to be nice to you." Marcus scrolled through Netflix, trying to settle on something for us to watch.

I stopped what I was doing and turned to my friend. "You said that to her? You told her that you wouldn't marry her unless she could be nice to me?"

"I absolutely told her that. You're the best friend I've ever had, Willow, and I made it very clear to her that you were always going to be a huge part of my life." Marcus dropped the remote control on the couch and came back into the kitchen. "Are you surprised to hear that or something?"

"Yeah, I guess I am." I was actually more than a little surprised to hear that Cinnamon's attitude toward me was a deal breaker for Marcus marrying her.

"Why is that so shocking? You have to know by now how important you are to me. You were the best woman at my wedding, for goodness' sake," Marcus reminded me.

"Yeah, I guess I was. Thanks, Marcus," I said quietly, suddenly overcome by my own emotions.

"Thanks for what?" He placed one hand on my shoulder and tilted my head up to look at him with the other.

"Thanks for being my friend. Other than Tate, I've never been very important in anyone else's life, including my father's. I guess it makes me just a little bit emotional to hear that you feel that way about me." I swallowed hard and cleared my throat, trying to get my crazy feelings under control. Obviously, I was in love with Tate, but being close to Marcus always sent my pulse racing. I reminded myself that it was a physical response, nothing more.

"Well, you're very important in my life." Marcus smiled sweetly at me.

Breaking eye contact, I turned back to the stove to finish our meal. "This is almost ready. Go have a seat and I'll bring it to you."

After mixing in the ingredients, the pasta was ready to be served. The savory aroma wafted into my nostrils, and my mouth salivated in response. *I sure do know how to cook.* Dishing up two heaping plates full of food, I carried them into the living room, handed one to Marcus, and then settled on the couch next to him with my own. I shoveled an obscenely large spoonful into my mouth and sighed contentedly.

"This is amazing," Marcus mumbled with his mouth full. "I wish Cinnamon could cook like this. Heck, I wish Cinnamon could cook at all."

"Don't you guys have a personal chef?" I asked, already knowing the answer.

"Of course we do. We also have a maid, a gardener, a pool boy, a few bodyguards, and a butler. I was told that they came with the mansion that Cinnamon's parents bought us as a wedding present," Marcus answered with a smirk.

"Then why don't you ask your personal chef to cook something for you? I'm pretty sure he or she could whip up some mac and cheese," I countered playfully.

"I gave all the staff the week off. I'm not used to ordering people around, and I don't like that my house is always filled with strangers. As soon as Cinnamon left for London, I told them to do whatever they wanted for a week. When she comes home, she can tell them to come back to work." He shrugged.

I nodded in understanding. "I know what you mean. I grew up surrounded by staff at Dad's house, so I never really thought much about it until I lived on my own. Now I can say without a doubt that it would drive me crazy to always have people around, messing in my business. It sounds to me like you're having a hard time adjusting to the lifestyles of the rich and famous. The high life isn't all it's cracked up to be, huh?"

"It's been an adjustment, for sure. I mean, I'm used to living in a one-bedroom apartment, and now I live in a house that's so big I practically need GPS and a Maps app to find my way around. Don't get me wrong, it was really generous of Cinnamon's parents to buy us the house. I'm not complaining."

"I know you're not complaining. But let's be honest, it wasn't generosity that made her parents buy you two a house. It was their pride and their daughter's spoiled nature.

Can you imagine Cinnamon living in your little apartment? Making her own meals? Cleaning her own messes? I know I can't." I wasn't trying to belittle her, but I knew Cinnamon just as well as Marcus did, if not better. She had never taken care of herself, and she wouldn't have survived ten minutes without staff to see to her needs.

"She is a spoiled princess. I'll be the first to admit it. The truth is I knew what I was getting into when I made her my wife, and I love her anyway. And it's not exactly a hardship to live in a mansion and have people waiting on me hand and foot. But it is nice to just hang out here at your place and be myself for a while. So thanks." Marcus continued eating his pasta.

"You know you're welcome here any time." I actually felt a bit sorry for Marcus. I knew how much he loved Cinnamon, but they were two very different people from two vastly disparate backgrounds. They were going to have to work extra hard to make their marriage last.

"So tell me about work. Did you have any responses to your Help Wanted sign today?" Marcus finished his pasta and set the plate on the coffee table.

"I had some inquiries, but nothing serious. A few people said they were going to tell their friends that I was hiring," I said between bites of mac and cheese.

"I think it's great that you're so busy you need to hire an employee. Are you still hoping to buy a delivery bike?"

"That's the plan, as soon as I find the right person to work for me. I'm hoping that whoever I hire can work a couple of shifts in the food truck and also be the main delivery person. We both know I shouldn't be the one riding the delivery bike. That's just a disaster waiting to happen."

Marcus leaned back on the couch and laced his fingers together behind his head. Omelet rose from her cat bed across the room, jumped onto the couch, and curled up next to him. She really thought Marcus was the best thing since sliced bread. She wasn't wrong. "Yeah, you might be my best friend, but you're a total klutz. You have no business riding a bike through Portland."

"Thanks for the vote of confidence." I smirked.

"What are friends for? Anyway, I'm happy to help you shop for a delivery bike if you need it. I know a few people with some connections, so just let me know."

"That would be great." I finished eating and set my plate beside Marcus's. "So, what are we watching tonight? I was telling Tate about that new cat documentary. Are you up for it?"

"Sure, whatever you want," he replied good-naturedly.

I clicked Play on the cat documentary, snuggled back on the sofa, and turned off the overhead light. Marcus and I sat in companionable silence as the light from the television flickered in the dark room. Omelet was fast asleep, and I could already feel my eyes getting droopy. There was no way I was going to last until the end of the show, but that was all right. I could finish it another time.

I glanced over at Marcus, who looked perfectly at home on my sofa. He had really come to mean a lot to me over the past year, and I had a hard time remembering when he wasn't in my life.

Sure, he was gorgeous, and being around him caused my heart to race and my pulse to quicken, but I was used to that by now. Marcus and I were both in love with other people. Tate was crazy to be worried about me spending time with him.

Wasn't he?

CHAPTER FOUR

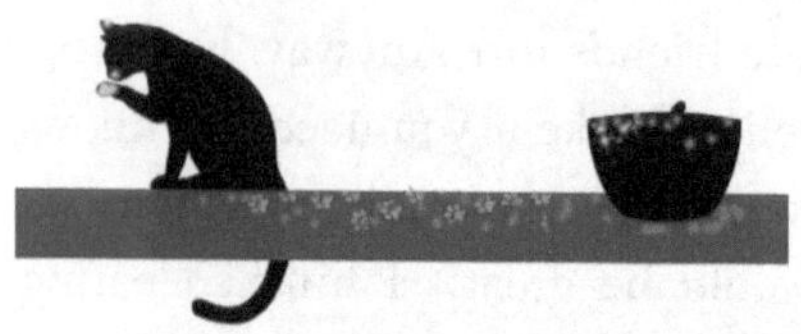

"Willow, you're going to have to move. My arm is cramped."

I moaned, adjusted myself, and snuggled closer to Tate. Our limbs were intertwined, and I was so comfortable. There was nothing better than waking up next to the man I loved.

"You have to get up. You're drooling on me."

I squirmed again but didn't open my eyes. Taking a deep breath, I inhaled the scent of lingering cologne and let the smell permeate my nostrils.

My eyes flew open in confusion. *That is not what Tate smells like!* Turning my head, I saw Marcus's face next to mine. Startled, I backhanded him so hard that his head snapped back from the force.

Fully awake at that point, I jumped off the couch, staring in horror while Marcus howled in pain as blood gushed from his cut lip. "Oh no! Oh, Marcus, I'm so sorry."

I ran to the kitchen and grabbed a dish towel. Rushing back to kneel in front of him, I dabbed at the blood on my friend's lip as I apologized profusely.

"Why did you hit me? All I did was ask you to move." Marcus glared at me from behind the towel.

"You startled me! Why were we sleeping together on my couch? I can't remember anything! What happened between us last night?" Confusion mixed with embarrassment tangled in my brain as I tried to come to grips with the idea that I hadn't spent the night with Tate. Instead, I'd been snuggling with Marcus!

How did I let that happen?

"Why are you overreacting? Nothing happened between us. We fell asleep watching the cat documentary. You need to calm down," Marcus mumbled as he continued to apply pressure to his busted lip.

"Overreacting? Marcus Tucker, I am not overreacting. I never overreact," I shot back at him as I paced back and forth across my living room floor.

Oh, what have I done? How will I ever explain this to Tate?

I glanced at Omelet, who eyed me suspiciously. Obviously she knew the truth.

Just calm down for a second and think of this rationally, Willow. You fell asleep on Marcus, thinking he was Tate. That's an innocent, honest mistake, right?

Somehow I knew that if Tate had walked in and found us that way, he would think it was anything but innocent or honest.

Guilt gnawed at me, and I tried to ignore it. Maybe nothing had happened besides sleeping. That was possible, right?

Sure, Willow. You just spent the night tangled up with a handsome man all alone in your apartment and nothing happened. Right!

The truth of the matter was that Tate would think

something had happened if he'd found us, and that's all that mattered. I also knew what Cinnamon would think.

They cannot find out about this! Ever!

"Marcus, I already know the answer to this, but I just have to make sure. Do you swear nothing happened between us besides sleeping?" I eyed him closely, trying to detect any inkling of deception. My heart raced so fast that I was having a difficult time thinking rationally.

"Willow, nothing happened. Don't you think you would remember if it had? I mean, give me a little more credit than that. I assure you that it's not something you would forget." Marcus winked at me teasingly and my face flushed.

His lip had stopped bleeding, but my backhanded wake-up call was definitely going to leave a mark. I felt terrible all over again. Luckily Cinnamon wasn't due home for several more days. His injury should be healed by then.

"I'm sorry. You're right. I'm overreacting. I know nothing happened between us, but it was just so shocking to wake up next to you... like... that." I swallowed hard, because if I was being honest with myself, I had felt right at home in his arms.

I am a horrible, awful fiancée. Am I allowing myself to get too close to Marcus?

I loved Tate, but the truth was Marcus and I had always shared a strong bond. We'd kissed on a couple of occasions, and we had come pretty close to doing more before I'd made up my mind between him and Tate.

Although my conscious mind thought of him as just a friend, did I subconsciously think otherwise? *The whole idea is ridiculous!* Tate was my fiancé, and Marcus was my friend—nothing more, nothing less. I was reading far too much into the situation. It was all just a big mistake.

I heard my phone chime in the bedroom, and knowing I

needed to step away from Marcus for a few minutes, I headed in that direction. I took a calming breath and grabbed my phone off the nightstand to check the text message. Of course it was from Tate, so I answered right away.

Tate: Morning, babe. I'm getting off work soon. Some of the guys from the fire station are going on a hike today. Will you come with me?
Willow: Hiking? Me? Are you serious? What about work?
Tate: You need a break. Close the truck for the day. The guys said the trail is really easy. You'll be fine.
Willow: I guess I could use a break…
Tate: I'll be home in an hour and we'll leave after that. I promise to take care of you on the hike.
Willow: Okay. I hope you know what you're getting us into.

I sighed and dropped the phone onto my bed. It was barely morning, and things had already gone from bad to worse. *At this rate, I might not even make it through the day.*

Hiking? What is Tate thinking? What a crazy thing to suggest we do.

Hiking had the potential to be disastrous for me. I wasn't exactly what anyone would call an "outdoorsy" type of girl. Come to think of it, I was the polar opposite. My idea of an outside activity was running from shady spot to shady spot on a sunny day. I thought nature was great, just as long as I was watching it from inside an air-conditioned building. Outside was hot and dirty, full of bugs and other kinds of creepy-crawly things that I'd rather not encounter.

I couldn't believe I'd just agreed to go into the woods.

Any other time, I would have flat-out refused to go hiking, but agreeing to participate in an activity that Tate enjoyed every once in a while was the right thing to do. He always did nice things for me, and it was great that I was returning the favor.

Yeah right, Willow. You know exactly why you're doing this, and it's not out of the kindness of your heart. I was no saint. I was doing it for completely selfish reasons. It was out of guilt, not because I wanted to be a good fiancée. *I really am a poor excuse for a human being.*

Oh well, if nothing else, it would give us all a good laugh. A nice walk in the forest would make everything better.

A waft of cologne pulled me away from my thoughts and reminded me that my clothes still smelled like Marcus. *Smelling like another man will go over like a lead balloon with Tate.* I dropped my clothes into the bottom of the hamper, then covered them with the rest of the pile. After burying my guilt with the dirty clothes, I took a quick shower and threw on my robe.

I heard a sound in the living room and realized that Marcus was still in the apartment. I'd been so preoccupied with the thought of hiking that I'd forgotten he was there. I needed to make sure he was long gone before Tate arrived. If he showed up and figured out what had happened, my ship was sunk, and so was Marcus's. I could not let Tate find out that I'd spent the whole night with his nemesis.

Marching out into the living room, I found Marcus lying on the couch, still holding the towel to the lip I'd bloodied.

"Marcus, it's time for you to get up and get out of here. I'm so sorry I smacked you across the face this morning, and normally I would cook you a really great breakfast to make up for it, but that isn't happening today," I rushed out.

"Look, I promise nothing happened." Marcus touched his lip gingerly and attempted to get his bearings.

"Yeah, sure, fine, whatever. Nothing happened, but you need to go home now." I smiled tensely and tapped my foot, hoping he would snap to it.

"I know. I was hoping to stop bleeding first." Marcus gazed at me in confusion, probably trying to understand why I was such a lunatic.

"Tate is on his way home, and you don't need me to tell you how much he's going to hate finding you here this morning. Get my drift?" I clapped my hands briskly. "Chop, chop."

"Got it. But you do know we're going to have to talk about this little mishap eventually, right?" Marcus grabbed his keys from my coffee table and hugged me quickly.

"No, really, Marcus, we don't ever have to talk about it. There's nothing to talk about. As a matter of fact, let's make a pact to *never speak of this again*." I looked him directly in the eyes, hoping to convey my point.

I wanted nothing more than to forget the latest embarrassing episode of the Willow show. Mostly, I just wanted to deal with this situation like I did most things—by ignoring them and hoping they would go away.

"Willow—"

"No. Never again. We're wiping it from our memories. Last night never happened." I smiled tensely.

"Whatever you say, crazy lady. Thanks for dinner, and thanks for keeping me company. Sorry about all this. I'll call you later."

"Don't apologize. You didn't do anything wrong. We just fell asleep. But Tate and Cinnamon would definitely not understand. And I really am sorry for hitting you." I hugged him quickly, kissed the end of my fingertip, and touched his lip lightly.

It looks so painful. I really hurt him. I wonder how he's going to explain his messed-up face at work today.

Without another word, Marcus was gone. I decided there was nothing else for me to do but move on and forget about it.

After I cleaned up the mess in my living room, I went back into my bedroom to try to figure out what I should wear.

What did a girl wear to go hiking? Knowing I didn't have anything in my closet that even remotely resembled something a person might find in an REI catalog, I was going to have to do what I did best—improvise.

I searched my closet and grabbed a pair of brightly colored, floral-patterned leggings. *Leggings are stretchy and comfortable, and flowers grow in nature, so they must be appropriate for hiking.* I paired them with a flowy, canary-yellow cotton tunic that matched the color of the flowers, then tied an emerald green bow around my ponytail.

Now for shoes. I obviously didn't own any hiking boots, but I did have my trusty ruby-red, knee-high Doc Martens. They would have to do. I slipped my feet into them and prayed I'd make it through the day without any blisters.

"Babe, I'm here," Tate called. I heard him shut the apartment door behind him.

"I'm in the bedroom getting dressed," I answered, swallowing hard and trying to appear innocent.

"Missed you last night." He wrapped me in a hug and greeted me with a kiss.

"Missed you too," I replied before kissing him again. I worked hard to push down the guilt.

I loved Tate so much, and I didn't want there to be any secrets between us. I would never do anything to hurt him intentionally. I knew I should just tell him what happened with Marcus, but that would do nothing but make him even more suspicious than he already was. So I kept my mouth shut about having spent the entire night with the guy who made Tate see green. Instead, I changed the subject.

"So... hiking. Are you sure you know what you're getting into by taking me out into nature?"

"It'll be fine, babe. The guys said it's a really easy trail. One of them even took their two-year-old on it last month, so you should be able to do it with no problems." Tate stepped away from me and gave me a quick once-over. "Is... uh... is that what you're wearing?"

"Yes. I know they're not technically hiking clothes, but they're the closest things I have. They're stretchy and comfortable. At least I didn't wear a dress." I smiled.

"You've got a point. And you put on boots instead of your Birkenstocks. You're nearly a professional hiker already." He smirked.

"I actually considered wearing my Birks, but I was afraid it might rain, and then my feet would be wet and cold. I put a lot of thought into my outfit." I put my hands on my hips and dared him to criticize my clothing choice.

"As always, you are absolutely perfect. I've just never seen anyone look so... colorful to go on a hike." Tate winked at me. "At least I won't lose you in the forest. Your bright clothing will be a beacon for me to follow."

"I'll be ready to go as soon as I get Omelet dressed," I replied as I sat on the bed and finished tying my boots.

"We're taking Omelet?" Tate scrunched his nose and raised an eyebrow in question.

"Yes. I've had to leave her home alone more often than I've wanted to lately. If we're going to be gone all day, then she has to come with us."

"And you have to get her dressed because...?"

"Because we're going hiking! There will be bugs, and dirt, and grass, Tate. Omelet doesn't like to have her fur messed up. You know that." I rolled my eyes and wondered why I had to explain it to Tate. He knew how she was.

"All right, whatever you want," he conceded.

I knew exactly what she was going to wear. I'd been waiting for the right event, and hiking was the perfect occasion. Heading over to Omelet's dresser, I pulled out the outfit, then called her into the bedroom and began dressing her. She sat obediently while I pulled the clothing over her head and adjusted it on her body.

"Willow, what is *that*?" Tate asked as his eyes widened.

"It's a dirndl," I explained.

"A what?"

"A dirndl—a traditional dress worn in the Alps. We're climbing a mountain, so it seems only natural for her to dress appropriately."

"You're putting the cat in a Swiss dress and taking her hiking with us? I love you, Willow, but there is absolutely nothing normal about that." Tate laughed so hard that tears streamed down his face.

"Hmm... seems normal to me." I shrugged. "I'm not sure why you think it's strange."

"That is exactly why I love you so much." Tate grabbed Omelet's leash, attached it to her collar, and we headed out the door to become one with nature.

CHAPTER FIVE

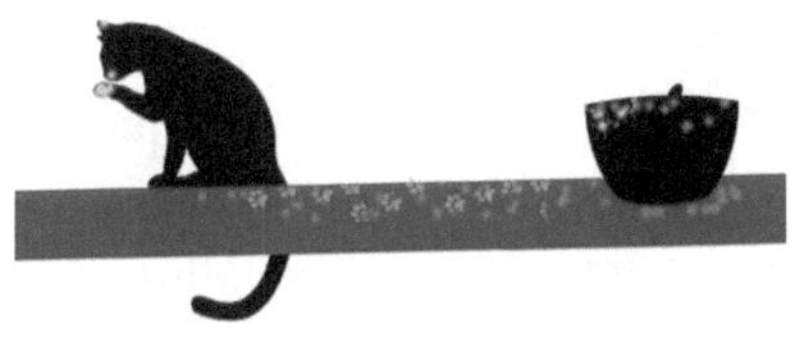

Tate walked a few steps ahead of me, laughing with his fellow firemen as we wound our way up the trail. I swatted at a mosquito that had landed on my arm and simultaneously shooed away a fly that had been following me for at least a hundred yards. I wished I'd veiled my entire body in mosquito netting before leaving my house.

What's so great about the Great Outdoors anyway? I don't get it.

Personally, I had no idea why people enjoyed nature. Being outside was nothing short of torture. The only upside I could find was the fact that the trail was mostly shaded, so I didn't have to deal with the sun.

Tate, who was completely in his element, seemed to be having a great time. He was in deep conversation with the other three firefighters who had joined us on our little adventure. Not only was I the lone woman, but I was also the only one who didn't climb ladders and carry people out of burning buildings for a living. As I ambled up the hill, it was painfully obvious that I wasn't in all that great of shape, and my cardiovascular endurance left much to be desired.

I trailed behind the group because the steep incline was wreaking havoc on my asthma, and I'd stupidly left my inhaler at home. However, I didn't want anyone else to know that. I was light-years outside of my comfort zone, but I didn't want to embarrass Tate in front of his friends by being a whiner. Instead, I trudged on.

An obnoxiously loud owl hooted in the distance, and I practically jumped out of my skin. I squealed loudly as I tripped over a large boulder in my path and went sprawling onto the ground, narrowly avoiding falling on poor Omelet. She glared at me as I lay on my back, panting and staring up at the forested canopy above.

"Sorry, baby. I would never squash you on purpose. I'm just not cut out for this hiking thing," I apologized to Omelet, who looked so adorable in her dirndl that I forgot my problems for a second and simply admired her.

"Babe, are you all right?" Tate had apparently heard the ruckus and observed me falling head over feet. He rushed back and knelt on the ground beside me.

"I'm just peachy. In fact, I've never been better. I love hiking." I tried to keep the sarcasm out of my voice, but that was an exercise in futility.

"Grab my hands and I'll help you up." Tate rose to his feet and hoisted me once again to a standing position. "You hate every second of this, don't you?"

"Who, me? Don't worry about me. I love this. Yay, nature!" I shook my fists in the air like I was a forest cheerleader or something equally ridiculous. "It's good to get out of your comfort zone every once in a while, right? I'll be flitting around like a woodland nymph before the day's over." I smiled widely and tried to make the ridiculous words sound convincing.

It's amazing the things a girl will do because of a guilty conscience.

Tate deserved to enjoy himself, even if I would rather brush Omelet's teeth than endure another second of the hike. He rarely got to do activities that he liked because I was so whiny and unadventurous; he always insisted we do things I wanted to do instead.

Trying to be selfless, I reminded myself that I was a strong woman. Tate should have the opportunity to finish the afternoon with his friends, and I decided the horrible hiking debacle wasn't going to get the best of me.

Besides, we've been out here for over an hour already. How long could it possibly last?

"Did you just say, 'yay, nature'?" Tate looked curiously at me.

My sunny disposition was obviously setting off warning bells in his mind. He knew I didn't want to be out there. I couldn't get anything past him.

"Well, you know, if you can't beat 'em, join 'em, right? I'm out here, so I might as well make the best of it." I flashed him a toothy grin for good measure.

"If you're sure...," Tate said cautiously. "You know, any time you want to leave, just tell me and we'll go back, okay?"

"We are hiking this trail to the end." I stood on my tiptoes and kissed his cheek. "How far might that be, by the way?"

"It's just another five miles up, then a quick hike back. We should be done before nightfall. But I'll stay back with you and we can take it slowly." Tate wrapped his arm around my shoulders. "Hey, guys, you go on ahead. We'll catch up in a bit," he called to his friends.

Before nightfall? I will surely die in the godforsaken wilderness before nightfall. And Tate apparently thinks that spending the day in a mosquito-infested hell is perfectly enjoyable.

How did I get myself into this situation? Oh yeah, I spent the night in the arms of another man, that's how!

Oblivious to my mental conversation, Tate continued, "By the way, one of the guys said he has a buddy who sells custom-made bicycles. He said he could hook you up with his friend's name, and he can build you a delivery bike. You could get a great deal." Tate clasped my hand in his and we continued up the trail together.

I squeezed it and tightened my grip on Omelet's leash in my other hand. "That's amazing news! See, this day just keeps getting better, right?"

"Indeed it does. By the way, I forgot to ask what you and Marcus did last night," Tate said offhandedly.

"What do you mean? What would Marcus and I do? We didn't do anything," I stammered as I stopped walking. Omelet looked at me with wide eyes, probably trying to warn me to keep my big mouth shut.

"Okay, that was a strange reaction, even for you." Tate eyed me suspiciously and looked as if he was going to ask me a question.

My heart raced inside of my chest. *He knows! He somehow found out that Marcus was my cuddle partner last night, and he's trying to make me confess!* I took a deep breath and tried not to incriminate myself even more. "There's nothing strange about my reaction. Your question was strange. Why would you ask what Marcus and I did last night?"

"Because you mentioned that he might come over." Tate shrugged.

"Oh yeah, he came over. No big deal. Nothing to report." I turned and started walking up the trail again. Tate followed after hesitating for a second.

"Apparently I've missed something, but I'm just going to let this one rest for now because you're clearly not going to fill me in." Tate grabbed my hand once again, and we walked for a few more minutes in silence.

Get a handle on yourself, woman! If Tate doesn't already know you're guilty as sin, he's going to figure it out soon enough if you keep babbling on like an idiot.

Taking a deep breath, I tried desperately to find some enjoyment in the wretched hiking experience. I watched as a small bird circled overhead before landing on a tree branch above me. I wasn't sure what species of bird it was, but it was sort of pretty.

As I admired its colorful feathers, I felt Omelet tug on her leash. She lunged toward the trunk of the tree and would have climbed it in a split second if I hadn't pulled her back. Apparently, she thought the bird was her own personal lunch delivery.

"Omelet, you're not going to eat that bird, so you can push the thought right out of your mind. I don't have the time or the fire-building skills to cook it for you, and I'm certainly not letting you eat it raw," I scolded.

Omelet hissed at me in response, and I was about to give her a long list of reasons why I wouldn't let her eat the bird when I felt a strange, wet, oozing sensation on my head. Placing my hand in my hair, I squealed out loud as I felt the gooey stickiness. I pulled my hand away and saw it was coated in a grayish-white, slimy substance.

"What is that?" I looked at Tate, desperately hoping that it was anything other than what I suspected it to be.

"Uh, that would be bird poop, Willow," Tate answered as he tried not to laugh.

"Bird poop? A bird pooped on my head? Ewww!" I

squealed again and stomped my feet in frustration, glaring at the small bird I'd been admiring only minutes before. Shaking my fist in the air, I yelled, "I should have let my cat eat you for lunch!"

"Here, babe, let me help you." Tate reached into his backpack and pulled out a towel, dabbing gently at the offensive poop on my head. When he realized it wasn't going to come off easily, he pulled out his canteen, dumped a bit of water onto the towel, and rubbed harder. "There you go. You're as good as new."

"Hardly. I can't believe that bird pooped on my head. I hate nature, and clearly nature hates me," I sulked.

"You've had enough. Let's go home," he suggested.

"No, we're seeing this thing through to the bitter end," I said stubbornly. "I do have to use the bathroom, though. Where might I find one?"

"Look around, babe. The world is your bathroom." Tate spread his hands widely and grinned at the look of horror I knew was on my face.

"You mean I have to do it out here?" I couldn't imagine anything more humiliating than squatting out in the open to do my business.

"Well, not out here. You go behind a bush or something." He was trying very hard not to laugh at my ignorance of surviving the wilderness.

"All right, I'll just go find a nice big bush to squat behind, then. No problem at all." I smirked.

"Do you want me to come with you?"

"You stay here with Omelet. I'll be back." I handed Omelet's leash to Tate and trudged through the trees. Glancing over my shoulder, I saw him standing a few feet away on the trail. I was still too close. I needed to keep going if I didn't want to give him a show.

Wandering a bit farther until I could no longer see him, I scanned my surroundings, looking for the perfect bush. *I can't believe I'm about to pee behind a bush. What has my life become?* When I found one that offered the right amount of cover, I did what I'd come to do. I wasn't sure what I was supposed to use in place of toilet paper, and I wanted nothing more than some hot, soapy water to wash my hands, as well as my hair. Both toilet paper and soap were luxuries that weren't afforded to me in the Great Outdoors.

I cannot wait until this day is over. I swear it can't get any worse than this.

I finished my business and walked back in the direction from which I'd come—at least, I thought it was the same direction. But as I continued, I started to doubt my steps. I looked around for some sort of landmark to tell me that I was going the right way, but I had no idea what that might be. I couldn't see Tate. The trees all looked the same, and I couldn't spot any footprints in the leafy foliage below.

Is this the way I came? Or was it the other way? Doubting myself, I turned and went in the opposite direction. After walking several steps, though, I realized that wasn't the right way either.

Panic began to set in. *I'm lost! I'm lost and I'm going to die!*

My breath came hard and fast, and my heart began to race. Suddenly, the rustling of leaves made me jump. I turned just in time to see a furry squirrel scurry up the trunk of a nearby tree.

That could just as easily have been a bear! A bear is going to come along and eat me for his dinner. I'm going to die out here in the wilderness, and no one is going to know where to find me!

I tried to reorient myself, but it was no use. I'd obviously wandered miles away from the trail and I was officially lost. Of all the places for me to go missing, it would have to be out there in the wasteland! I didn't know how to survive. I had no food, no water, and my cell phone had no reception. I would starve to death. What would I do when it grew dark? I would go crazy alone in the forest. Once the sun went down, my limbs would be torn from my body by a ravenous wolf or bear.

Panting heavily, I spun around in a circle. *How long have I been lost? Has it been hours? It must have been several hours by now.* I missed Tate and Omelet desperately. *What if I never see them again?* My brain was racing a thousand miles per hour. *I'm so hungry. I'm probably dehydrated. I'm going to die!*

I'd worked myself into a complete frenzy by that time. As thoughts of my certain demise began to buzz around in my brain, tears slid down my cheeks. *I have to get out of here! I have to get help!*

I began screaming as loudly as I could. "Tate! Tate, please help me!"

I screamed at the top of my lungs, and Tate and Omelet came running toward me. When he saw me, Tate stopped cold. "You scared me to death. What on earth are you screaming about?"

So grateful that he'd been able to find me, I ran to him and threw myself into his arms. "Oh, Tate, I knew you would find me. I knew you wouldn't ever give up. Omelet, I knew you wouldn't let him stop looking."

"Stop looking? What do you mean? Why are you so sweaty?" The questions continued while Tate's face registered confusion.

"I got lost when I went to the bathroom. I wandered

around for hours, and then it got so hot... I couldn't find you, and there was a bear... well, I guess it was technically a squirrel, but it could have been a bear," I babbled on while Tate just stared at me.

I squeezed him again as the reality of the situation crashed down on me. He had saved my life. "How long have you been looking for me?"

"Willow, you've been gone for less than five minutes. You went behind the bush to use the bathroom. What are you talking about?"

"Five minutes? Is that all? It seemed like hours. It's not possible," I stammered.

"Babe, I promise you were never lost. I could hear you walking around over here. I was just trying to give you some privacy to do your business." The corners of Tate's mouth quivered and threatened to upturn.

"I wasn't lost? I sure felt lost. And I was so hot...." I shrugged, suddenly embarrassed. Apparently my overactive imagination had gotten the best of me once again.

"Well, you got the hot part right, at least. Lucky for you, I'm a fireman, so I know just how to handle hot." Tate leaned down and kissed me deeply. "And now we're all alone in the woods, so...."

Wrapping my arms around Tate's neck, I pulled his face toward mine and nestled myself deeper into his arms. "Thanks for finding me, even if I wasn't really lost."

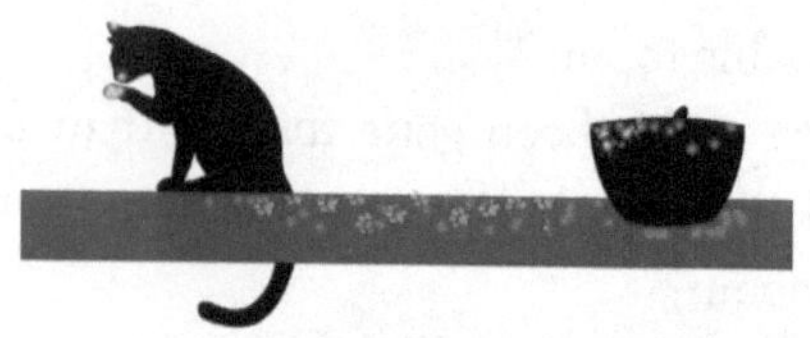

CHAPTER SIX

Omelet and I hopped off the MAX early the next morning and hurried toward the Dancing Crêpe. I held a steaming butterscotch latte in one hand and Omelet's Feline Frother in the other, which I planned to dump into her bowl once we arrived. After the exhausting hiking fiasco the day before, I was beat.

Unfortunately, on top of being worn out, I'd also returned from the forest with a couple of unwanted souvenirs. I had a rash on my arms, courtesy of coming into contact with stinging nettles, and I was sporting a quarter-sized mosquito bite on the back of my neck. If I never went into the woods again, it would be too soon.

Because I was still groggy from the dose of Benadryl I'd taken the night before, I'd slept through my alarm. As a result, I hadn't had time to sit down and visit with Suzanne at Simpson Coffee like I usually did. Pressed for time, Omelet and I took our caffeine to go.

We arrived at the food truck, and I placed my coffee on the step while I unlocked the door. I liked getting to work much earlier than we did that day, so I knew I would be rushing to be ready by opening time. Pouring Omelet's Frother into her dish, I unhooked her leash, and she headed to her little home in the corner. She knew she had to stay out of sight when she came to work with me.

I prepared crêpe batter, chopped some fruit and vegetables, took stock of my supplies, and made a quick inventory list. I would need to make a shopping trip soon, and I had several after-hours catering events coming up in the next couple of months. The pressure to find an employee was really starting to stress me out. As much as I didn't want to be anyone's boss, I knew it was quickly becoming necessary. I was hanging on by my claws, like a cat in a tub full of water.

Before I knew it, opening time was upon me. I turned on the blinking sign, and the line began to form almost immediately. I smiled at my customers and pumped out crêpes as quickly as my tired hands could move.

"You make that look pretty easy," said the twentysomething girl with purple hair and a pierced eyebrow who was next in line.

"Well, it's not easy, but it's not rocket science either," I replied with a grin. "What can I get for you?"

"I'll have the Pirouette and a job application," she answered with a shrug.

"A job application?" The request stopped me in my tracks.

"Yeah, your sign says Help Wanted, or is that just for decoration?" The girl raised her pierced eyebrow in question.

"No, that would be an awful decoration, wouldn't it? It's not even a well-made sign," I rambled on, startled by her request. I was so inexperienced that I hadn't even thought of printing off an application.

"So, like, are you still looking for help?" She cocked her purple head to the side impatiently and fidgeted with the buttons on her black dress.

"Yes, I am looking for help," I hedged.

"Uh... should I fill out the application in person, or do you have it posted online somewhere?" The girl's face registered both irritation and confusion at my obvious lack of knowledge about my own hiring process.

I am so bad at this. What was I thinking? Of course I would need to have potential employees fill out a job application. Everyone knows that!

"Well, you see, I just posted the sign and I... forgot to bring the... applications with me. If you can just come inside and wait for a few minutes, we can talk about what I'm looking for. Just let me get through the line and I'll be right with you. You can... just eat your crêpe while you wait...." I fumbled my words awkwardly.

"Whatever, I guess I can wait," she replied with an uninterested shrug.

I opened the door for her and led her inside. She took a seat in the only chair I had and grabbed her cell phone out of her bag. I returned to the counter, prepared her Pirouette, placed it into her hands, and went back to work.

She devoured the crêpe as I waited on customers. It wasn't long before the line had died down, so I turned my attention back to the girl. She appeared bored as she scrolled through her phone. She must have been sending a text, her blue-polished fingernails flying like colorful butterflies across the screen.

Leaning against the counter, I took a deep breath and tried not to sound like I had no idea what I was doing. "So, my name is Willow, and I'm the owner of the Dancing

Crêpe. I've been running it alone since I opened it, so the whole employee thing is new for me," I began.

"Did you want me to fill out that application?" she asked as she glanced up from her phone.

"About that... I was thinking we would just do an in-person application, if that's all right with you," I answered nervously.

"Sure, whatever. You're the boss." She shrugged and dropped her phone into her bag.

"Tell me a little bit about you."

"My name is Melody Block, and I'm twenty. I just moved to Portland from San Francisco a few months ago. I'm going to art school, and I'm basically broke, so I need a job like pronto. There's not much else to tell." She fidgeted in her chair and gnawed on her blue fingernails, a look of sheer boredom on her face.

"Well, business has really been picking up, so I need to hire an employee as soon as possible. I'm looking for someone who's able to work a few shifts in the truck, and also someone who can do my deliveries once I get a delivery bike. Do you have any type of relevant experience?"

"I've had a couple of customer service gigs. I worked part-time in a coffee shop in high school, and I'm a decent cook," she replied quickly, almost as if she'd rehearsed her answer.

Ignoring the warning bells in my brain, I continued. "Can you ride a bike?" I knew that what I really needed was someone who could do my deliveries, since I didn't want to do them myself. I was desperate to find that person.

"Sure, can't everyone ride a bike?" She eyed me with a touch of annoyance.

"Yeah, silly question, right? Who can't ride a bike?" I laughed loudly and tried to avoid making direct eye contact.

It's not like I can't ride a bike. I'm just really bad at anything that resembles exercise.

"So, when do you think I'll know if I got the job? I need one ASAP," Melody continued in a rush.

"How about if I let you know right now? Can you start today?" Relief mixed with a bit of apprehension flooded over me as I realized that I'd just hired my first employee.

"You mean you're going to hire me just like that? Don't you want some references or something?"

"Nah, that's okay." I waved her question aside as if I were shooing away a fly. "I don't need them." I grinned, although a little voice in the back of my mind was warning me to slow down.

"I've got to tell you, this is the weirdest job application process I've ever gone through," Melody said as she rolled her eyes.

"Well, that's Portland for you. We're all weird here!" I laughed nervously and prayed that I wouldn't live to regret my hastily made decision.

About that time, Omelet poked her head out of her carrier and gave Melody the once-over. She knew she wasn't supposed to be seen during business hours, so she slinked carefully along the wall in an attempt to be inconspicuous. She looked like a cat ninja, sneaking up on her prey.

The minute Melody spotted Omelet, her tough, annoyed demeanor changed. She even cracked a small smile. "Oh my goodness, what a cute little cat!" Melody dropped to her knees on the floor and made a little clicking noise at Omelet.

"Yeah, that's Omelet. Don't take it personally if she snubs you. She doesn't like very many people," I warned.

Rather than play hard to get, Omelet trotted right over

to Melody, sniffed her impatiently, curled up on the strange girl's lap, and purred loudly. My mouth flew open in shock.

"It doesn't look like that's going to be a problem. I guess she likes me." Melody cuddled Omelet on her lap and stroked her gray fur gently.

It should have made me happy that Omelet had given my new employee her stamp of approval, but instead a strange feeling came over me. Was it jealousy? Usually Omelet didn't like people until she got to know them a little better. She wasn't one to be so trusting. Neither was I, for that matter, and yet I'd just hired a complete stranger without even having her fill out a job application.

Had I just made a gigantic mistake in hiring the first person to inquire about the job? Suzanne had warned me several times that I absolutely should not hire a woman, and yet I'd gone and done exactly that.

Truth be told, Suzanne had a valid point. Unfortunately for me, I needed help immediately. I knew virtually nothing about Melody, but I was desperate. I couldn't handle all this on my own anymore.

Melody might not be the best person for the job, but she was the one who had applied. I could teach her everything she needed to know.

Besides, how bad could she possibly be if Omelet already liked her?

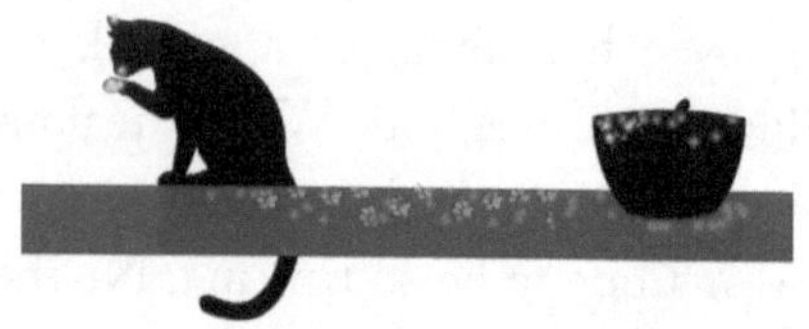

CHAPTER SEVEN

Exhaustion mingled with the lingering Benadryl fog in my brain as Omelet and I trudged down the hallway toward our apartment later that afternoon. Sadly, Melody's work ethic and people skills had proven to be less than stellar as we'd muddled through the rest of our shift together. By the end of the day, I wanted to punch myself in the face for hiring her on the spot.

What on earth was I thinking? This is precisely the reason that employers ask for references and inquire about work experience, Willow.

The annoying, purple-haired Melody didn't seem eager to work so much as she was eager to get her hands on her first paycheck. The first thing out of her mouth after hearing that she'd gotten the job was to inquire when she would be paid. When I'd told her that payday would be every other week and that tips were split between us, she rolled her eyes in exasperation and mumbled something under her breath that I'd assumed I was better off not knowing.

Within an hour of being trapped in the confined space with her, I knew I had made an awful mistake. She had no idea how to sift flour. When a customer came to the window, she rolled her eyes and said, "What do you want?" When the line got too long, she actually told a couple of customers that they should just go away and come back the next day. She didn't even know how to crack an egg.

I kept reminding myself that it had only been her first day. Maybe she was nervous. Certainly she would improve as we went along. *It's not like she can get any worse!* But oddly enough, in spite of Melody's sour mood, Omelet seemed quite smitten with her. I couldn't figure out why my usually finicky cat spent most of the day rubbing herself against Melody's legs and purring.

"Willow, dear, can you help me with these bags, please?" The lyrical voice behind me belonged to Nellie, the seventy-five-year-old woman who'd moved into Marcus's old apartment next door.

"Of course, Nellie. Let me grab them so you can unlock your door. You do have your keys, right?" I slipped Omelet's leash over my wrist, turned, smiled at my friend, and removed the two large paper grocery bags from her arms.

"You're such a sweet girl." Arms free of the burdensome parcels, Nellie pinched my cheeks lovingly before dangling her key in front of me with a smile and unlocking the door to her apartment. "You and Omelet come inside. I'll make you tea and a snack, and I'll give her some tuna."

"Are you sure, Nellie? I don't want to be any trouble to you," I began to protest, but she quickly shooed away my words.

"It's no trouble at all, darling girl. I'm a lonely woman, and you know I adore your company. Besides, I love spending time with Omelet," Nellie replied as she patted my arm and led me inside.

I placed the woman's groceries on her kitchen counter

and sighed with contentment as I looked at her cozy, inviting home. She had made Marcus's old apartment look like something out of a *Country Living* magazine. She displayed a collection of colored mason jars with various spices and ingredients on her kitchen counter, she always had lovely vases filled with wildflowers throughout the room, and it invariably smelled like something delicious had just finished baking in her oven. It was homey and charming, and I loved spending time with Nellie.

I unhooked Omelet's leash from her collar and collapsed into the chair at the grandmotherly woman's welcoming kitchen table. Omelet remained close to Nellie, anticipating the tuna snack that she'd grown accustomed to receiving when we visited our neighbor.

We'd officially met when I found the poor woman sobbing in the hallway shortly after she took up residence. She had been beside herself with worry over losing her keys, and she had no idea how to get inside of her new home. I took her into my apartment, introduced her to Omelet and Tate, fixed her a warm cup of tea, and called the apartment manager, who eventually came and let her in.

While I tried to calm her frazzled nerves, Tate obtained a new apartment key for her and made a spare copy to keep in my apartment in case an incident like that ever happened again. We became fast friends from that moment, and we visited with each other several times a week.

Nellie had lost her husband, Harold, only six months before she moved in. The couple had been married for fifty years, and this was the first time in her life that she had ever lived alone. It was obvious to me that she was overwhelmed by her new single status, and my heart ached for Nellie and the transition in which she found herself. I had loved her immediately, and I had no doubt that the feeling was mutual. Nellie's nurturing presence filled a space inside that I obviously needed, and I liked to think that I had a special place in her heart as well.

"Here you go, my dear," Nellie said as she served our tea. "I just made these scones this afternoon. You'll have to let me know what you think of the recipe."

I took a bite of the blueberry pastry and my taste buds applauded in appreciation. I had learned pretty quickly that Nellie was a talented baker, which was another thing we had in common. "Oh, Nellie, these are delicious."

"Thank you. It was my grandmother's recipe. She brought it with her from Scotland, and we've been using it in our family for years. That woman could bake better than anyone I've ever known—except maybe you, of course."

"You're one to talk, Nellie. You're a fabulous baker. I could learn a thing or two from you," I replied with my mouth full of scone.

"You know, I always wanted to open a bakery, but I just never got around to it. Of course, I suppose I was a little bit preoccupied with my husband and seven children." She chuckled as she sat down at the table with me.

"Yes, well, seven children would occupy anyone. I can't even imagine having one." Tate and I had discussed the subject of children several times, but the conversation always ended up dead in the water. I liked to believe that my maternal instincts were hidden in there somewhere, although I hadn't yet found them.

"Children are a gift, Willow. You'll understand someday when you and Tate get married and you have a few of your own." Nellie patted my hand lightly before biting into her scone.

"Yeah, I don't think so, Nellie. I'm pretty sure that's not going to happen. I can't really picture myself as a mother.

I'd be a mess, and I wouldn't want to do that to a kid." I raised my hand and shook my head at my friend.

"Why do you say that? I think you'd make a wonderful mother, Willow. Just look at how well you take care of your fur baby." Nellie gestured to Omelet, who was making short work of her bowl of tuna.

"I suppose that's true, but I don't know. Kids are different. My mom passed away when I was young, so I don't know the first thing about being one. All I've had are conniving, spoiled stepmothers, and I don't want to be anything like them. I'm not even that crazy about kids, to be honest. They freak me out a little bit. They're squirmy and sticky, and their eyes are too big." I shuddered as I thought about myself as a mother.

"Is this something you and Tate have talked about? You know, that fiancé of yours would make a fantastic father." Nellie sipped her tea as her blue eyes softened.

"Oh, there's no question about Tate's fatherly tendencies. He would be amazing. He really wants kids, too." I sighed as I thought about all the things Tate was willing to give up in order to be with me, possibly even the prospect of fatherhood. "Maybe that's why I'm stalling on planning our wedding. Maybe deep down I know I'm not the right girl for Tate." I shrugged as my eyes filled with tears.

I had never discussed my fears about marrying Tate with anyone, but Nellie had a way about her that caused me to open up. Besides the fact that the commitment and permanency of marriage scared me to death, the truth was I still believed that Tate was far too good for me. I knew I would always view myself as damaged goods.

"Darling, I've seen the two of you together. If there were ever a couple of true soul mates, it's you and your Tate.

Anyone with eyes can see that. There's so much love between the two of you," Nellie encouraged.

"Oh, we're not lacking in love. That's not what I mean at all. I just sometimes think I'm not good enough for him." I swallowed hard as I said the words out loud.

Immediately, I thought of the way I'd spent the night snuggled up with Marcus. I couldn't quite get past the guilt, and I wondered if I ever would.

No, I wasn't good enough for a man like Tate, and I knew it.

"Willow, you complement Tate in exactly the way he needs it, and he does the same for you. Besides, that man loves you fiercely, and you love him. Everything else is just details. You'll work it all out in time. Don't be afraid of true love, dear. Life means nothing without it." Nellie's eyes filled with tears, and I knew she was thinking about the loss of Harold.

"I love you, Nellie. I'm so glad we met." I rose from my chair and hugged her tightly.

I knew she was terribly lonely living on her own for the first time in her life. Her husband was gone, and her seven children were scattered all over the world. Her friendship had helped me so much already, and I wanted to help her however I could. The best way I knew was to just spend time with her.

"You're a dear, dear child. I couldn't ask for a better neighbor or a better friend." Nellie returned my hug.

Plopping back into my chair, I took another bite of the scone. "Oh yeah, I have some news. I hired my first employee today."

"You did? I'm happy for you, love. I know how worried you've been about finding the right person."

"Her name is Melody, and she's twenty. She recently

moved to Portland for art school." I thought about what a catastrophe she'd been that afternoon, and my head began to ache.

"She must have been pretty great to pull ahead of all the competition. I'm guessing you had a whole slew of applicants given the popularity of your food truck." Nellie smiled proudly at me.

"Yeah, well, about that...," I began.

"What's wrong?" Nellie's voice filled with concern.

"Well you see, I've never hired anyone before, and I sort of forgot about the application thing. So when she showed up and started asking about the job, I kind of just hired her on the spot." I rolled my eyes because saying it out loud only cemented the fact that I'd been ridiculously stupid for doing so.

"Oh my, that's a unique process." Nellie wrinkled her button nose and appeared to be contemplating her words before she spoke. I knew she was thinking how ridiculous I was, but she was far too kind to ever say it aloud.

"Oh, Nellie, it's not a process at all. It just goes to show that I should never be in charge of other people. This is exactly why I can never have children. Everything I touch turns into a disaster." I shook my head in embarrassment.

"Now just a moment. Don't get carried away." Nellie took a breath before she continued. "I'll admit that it was a bit hasty of you to hire a stranger on the spot. But you've done it now, and you'll just have to make the best of it. You'll have to teach her to be the kind of worker you want. I know you can do it, Willow. You're so much stronger than you give yourself credit for." Nellie patted my hand again.

"You have more confidence in me than I have in myself."

"I've lived a long time, Willow, and I've figured a few

things out. Sometimes we just need someone to believe in us when we can't believe in ourselves. It'll all work out. You'll see." Nellie's kind smile almost had me convinced that she was right. Almost.

"Sure, Nellie, it'll all work out. And if it doesn't, Melody and I will just end up killing each other. Or better yet, maybe she'll just rob me blind." I took the last sip of my tea and buried my head in my hands.

CHAPTER EIGHT

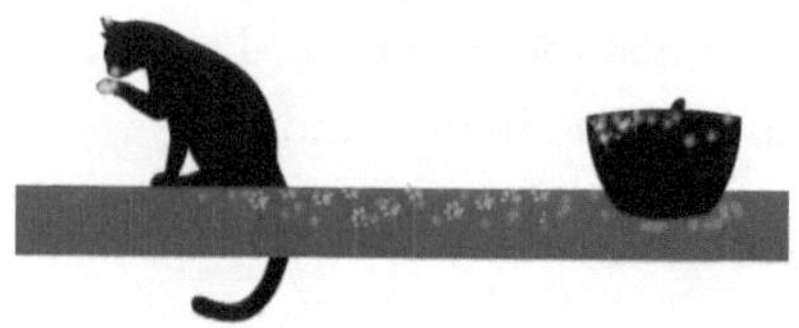

Two more miserable weeks passed by, and Melody's work ethic didn't improve. If anything, she was just as horrible, if not even more so, than she'd been on her very first day. I tried everything I could think of to inspire her to up her game, but she refused to learn.

She slogged along like a sloth in the food truck, taking far too long to take and prepare orders. She never smiled, and she acted like it was a chore to wait on customers. She messed up the recipes, made a disaster of the workspace, and never cleaned up after herself. Rather than lightening my load, Melody coming on board had created even more work for me.

Tate and Marcus thought it was crazy that I hadn't already fired her, and both men were taking bets on how long I could hold out without killing her. I would have sent her packing in a second, but I felt like I'd already wasted two weeks on "training" her. Even though I knew it was a long shot, I kept hoping that eventually she would catch on. I also didn't want to admit that I'd made a huge mistake on my first attempt to hire an employee.

I chopped some basil and tried to push all thoughts of Melody aside for the moment. My brand-new, custom-made delivery bike was arriving later that morning, and as much as I had wanted it, I really had no desire to ride the thing. I needed Melody to do that. I kept telling myself that as long as she could successfully make my deliveries, then the rest of it didn't matter.

I finished preparing the rest of the ingredients for that day's orders and turned on the Open sign. I'd told Melody not to come in until later that morning, not because I didn't need the help, but because I had to limit the time I spent with her each day in order to preserve my sanity. The delivery bike was supposed to show up any minute, and I wanted to savor the occasion alone. Purchasing the bike was a milestone for me and my business, and I wanted to experience it without Melody's sarcasm and black mood to dampen my special day.

I was sanitizing the counter when I heard an old-fashioned bicycle horn honking outside of the Dancing Crêpe. Popping my head out the window, I squealed with delight as I saw Jake, Tate's friend of a friend, strolling toward the food truck pushing the most gorgeous bike I had ever seen in my entire life.

The retro-reminiscent three-wheeled bike was seafoam green with bubblegum-pink trim. The tires were fat and wide, and the basket on the front was the same color as the trim. Pink and green streamers hung from the ends of the handlebars, and there was a chalkboard sign hanging from the basket that read "The Dancing Crêpe." Attached to the rear of the bike was a matching trailer with the food truck's name and phone number. The trailer itself was half refrigerated and half heated, so I could keep all orders at the perfect temperature. It had been expertly built to transport my creations.

"Oh, Jake, it's perfect! It's absolutely beautiful!" I clapped and squealed again as I opened the door and ran down the stairs excitedly.

He didn't seem at all surprised by my enthusiastic greeting, even though I'd only spoken to the man twice. He clearly knew that the bike was just what I'd envisioned, and he had probably anticipated my happy reaction.

"So it lives up to your expectations?" Jake grinned.

"It sure does. I can't believe you got it so exactly, perfectly right." I sighed in contentment. The bike was the realization of yet another one of my dreams, and the moment felt a little bit surreal.

"You made it easy, Willow. Very few people have the precise, detailed vision that you had for this bike. I knew just what to do from the way you described it to me." Jake motioned for me to sit on the pink seat, and I did.

I ran my hands over the fresh paint and fondled the streamers. The ability to make customized deliveries was going to take my business to the next level. Now I would be able to do it in style, and because of the trailer, I could load it up and not have to worry about the food perishing.

"You look pretty good on that thing. You're sure to get some attention." Jake winked.

"Oh, I won't be the one riding it. I'm a bit of a klutz, you see, so I'll have my employee do the deliveries. That's really the best thing for all parties involved." I giggled.

"Well, if your employee is even half as cute as you are, then it'll definitely give your business a boost." Jake's eyes twinkled at me.

"Th-thank you."

It was probably just my imagination, but it almost

seemed as if he was flirting with me. But that was crazy. After all, Jake was Tate's friend's friend, so he had to know I was engaged to Tate. He was just being nice to me, that's all.

It seemed like I was second-guessing everything these days. Ever since that night with Marcus, I was paranoid about doing anything that would even remotely hurt Tate's feelings. I couldn't handle any more guilt.

"I have to run, Willow. I'm really glad you're satisfied. Let me know if you need anything else. The bike is also under warranty. Everything is explained in the papers." Jake placed a large manila envelope in my hand and waved goodbye.

Once he was gone, I slid off the bike, congratulating myself that I'd avoided any injuries.

"What is that horrible-looking thing?" Melody's voice behind me made me cringe.

So much for the good vibes.

I took a deep breath, repeated my mantra that I would look horrible in an orange prison jumpsuit, and then turned around and plastered a smile on my face. "Good morning, Melody. This is my new delivery bike."

"You mean to tell me that you paid good money for that hunk of metal? It's ridiculous. It looks like an explosion happened at a rainbow factory." Melody wrinkled her nose in contempt.

Do not punch her in the face. Do not kill her. You would never survive in prison.

"I'm actually really pleased with the way it turned out, Melody. Jake did exactly what I asked him to do, and I think the happy colors represent me and the Dancing Crêpe well. Of course, you'll be the one riding it, so you'll need to at least pretend you like it." I worked hard to control my voice, which wasn't easy seeing as I would have preferred to slap the nasty girl right across the face.

"I cannot believe that I have to ride that thing. How embarrassing. I hope none of my friends see me on it." Melody let out an exasperated sigh and stomped inside the food truck.

"Shouldn't be a problem. I can't imagine you have any friends," I mumbled under my breath.

"Did you say something?" Melody asked, raising one pierced eyebrow in question.

"Nope, I was just talking to myself. I tend to do that a lot. Let's get to work."

We continued in silence for the next hour, which was probably for the best. Rather than work the window, I had Melody prepare an inventory list. If I wanted to keep the customers happy and returning to my food truck, I needed to keep my grumpy employee as far away from the general population as possible.

When the lunch rush died down, I grabbed the detailed list of instructions and delivery directions that I'd prepared the night before. I had painstakingly written down everything Melody needed to do and everywhere I needed her to make deliveries. Each order was labeled with a number that corresponded to the number on the map. The directions were foolproof. There was no way she could mess it up.

"Here is a map, detailed written instructions, the names and addresses of all the locations you'll be delivering to, and the contact person at each location. There are only five deliveries today. I figured we would start out light and add more once you get into the swing of things." I smiled as I handed her the packet.

"Ugh, there are five places I have to go? In just one

day?" Melody rolled her eyes and looked at me as if I'd asked her to ride the bike into outer space.

"Melody." I paused, counted to ten, and then continued. "Five deliveries in one day is nothing. It shouldn't even take you that long. Besides, this is precisely what you were hired to do."

"Yeah, whatever. I'll go do your stupid deliveries." She grabbed her purse and the instructions, then stormed out of the food truck.

My heart raced as I watched her climb angrily onto my beautiful delivery bike and ride away. *What a horrible, awful, wretched girl!* I would have stewed on it all a bit longer, but the line was starting up at the window again, and I had customers who wanted crêpes.

I worked through the rush and was tidying my workspace when I glanced at the clock. Melody had been gone for an hour and a half, and she hadn't called to ask any questions. The knots that had taken up residence in my stomach loosened a little bit, and I told myself that was a good thing. It meant the deliveries must have been going well.

Just then, my cell phone buzzed, and my heart sank as I saw Melody's phone number scroll across the screen. *I should have known it was all too good to be true.*

"Hey, Melody," I answered, trying to sound light-hearted.

"Is this some kind of joke? What are you trying to do, kill me?" Melody's angry voice took me by surprise. She was always a bit surly, but at that moment she sounded positively irate.

"Is that a trick question? Never mind. Calm down and tell me what you're talking about." I sighed deeply and told myself not to lose my cool.

"I'm talking about these stupid deliveries on this stupid

bike up and down these stupid hills!" she screamed into the phone. I pulled it away from my ear before she busted my eardrums.

"Okay." I swallowed hard, trying to figure out what I should say to her. "Are you telling me that you aren't able to do the deliveries, Melody?"

"I'm telling you that I refuse to ride up one more hill. I won't do it!"

"So what I'm hearing you say is that you only want to ride downhill, correct? That's not very practical for a bicycle delivery person." I was working hard to control the rage inside.

"Well, practical or not, I'm not doing it. You need to redo this map. You need to fix it so I don't have to go uphill anymore."

Enough is enough, Willow. You need to end this fiasco now. "Very well, Melody. Tell me where you are, and I'll come and fix everything."

Melody rattled off her location and I ended the phone call. Grumbling to myself, I hung a sign in the window that read "Be Back Soon," put Omelet on her leash, and headed to the nearest MAX stop. Ten minutes later, I jumped off the bus and saw Melody standing on the sidewalk next to my bike. She looked like she was ready to blow her top, and her cold eyes shot daggers at me as I approached.

"I cannot believe—"

I raised my hand to silence her before she could continue. "You're fired." Relief washed over me as I said the words I had been waiting to say for weeks.

"I'm what? You can't fire me!" She stomped her foot, and for a moment I thought she was going to punch me in the face.

"Oh, I can, and I did. I should have done it weeks ago.

No, I take that back. I should never have hired you in the first place." My resolve grew stronger as I realized that I was doing exactly what I needed to do.

No more Mr. Nice Guy!

"Well, I never—"

I held up my hand and cut her off mid-sentence once again.

"That's right, Melody. You never did much of anything. You didn't even try. All you've done is complain and whine and scare away my customers with your negative attitude. But it ends today. I hired you to do a job—bicycle delivery— and you've made it abundantly clear that you're unqualified to do that job. So you're fired."

"You're going to be sorry. You are going to pay for this, Willow Simpson. You're going to wish you'd never met me." Melody stepped closer to me and put her face directly in front of mine.

"Mission accomplished. I already wish I'd never met you." I smiled ruefully at her.

"Mark my words, you'll be sorry." Melody dropped the packet with the map and instructions on the sidewalk at my feet and stomped away in a huff.

As she retreated, I noticed something fall out of the pocket of her pants. I bent down to pick it up and gave it a sniff.

"It's a cat treat. No wonder you couldn't stay away from her, Omelet. She was bribing you with the cat treats she kept in her pockets." I bent down and gave Omelet a pat on the head. "We're lucky to be rid of her, but I do feel better knowing you didn't actually like her. I was getting kind of worried about your lack of judgment."

CHAPTER NINE

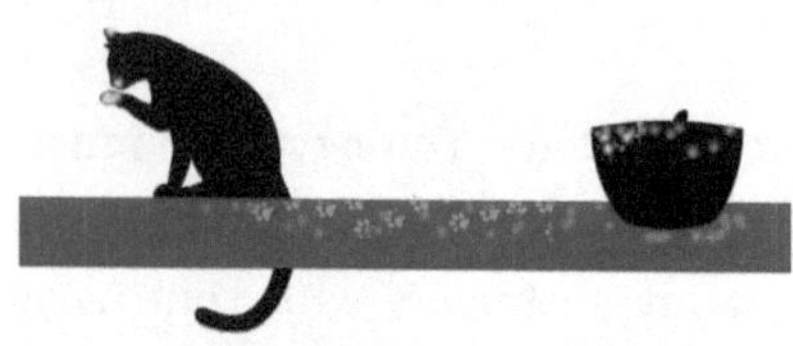

Somehow I made it through the next week without completely losing my mind. My work schedule wasn't any less hectic, and I was more aware than ever that I needed a break. Not only did I need it, but I needed it soon. Washing my hands of Melody had put me right back at square one; I felt desperate and overwhelmed.

I was cranky and unbearable to be around. The previous day I had yelled at Tate for eating the last slice of bread, and then later on, I snapped at him for leaving his duffel bag on the living room floor. The day before that, I'd called Marcus a "glutton for punishment" when he told me he was attending a charity event with Cinnamon. He argued that she was his wife and he wanted to give her his support, and I laughed at him and told him he was whipped. I was a poor excuse for a human being.

I had to hire someone new. Humming to myself, I taped the Help Wanted sign back into the window and straightened the stack of copies of the employment application that I'd found online the night before. *This time around, I'm going to take my time. Once bitten, twice shy, as they say.* It was better to be choosy than to quickly hire another dud.

The line at the food truck never slowed once that day, and by the time I got home, I was exhausted. My resolve to keep a positive attitude was quickly crumbling. I trudged down the hallway toward my apartment, hoping to get a bit of a rest before I had to go back out for a catering event. Weeks ago, I had scheduled it when I thought I had a bike rider who could assist.

All day long, I had tossed around the idea of whether or not I should cancel. I didn't want to do the event alone, knowing it would involve riding the bike to transport the food. The part of me that cared about my own safety thought canceling would be the best decision for all involved. But I couldn't cancel. Not following through with a contract was basically a death sentence for a small business. Word would get around quickly that I didn't fulfill my commitments, and it would be downhill from there.

With no other options, I had to do it all myself.

The venue was all the way across town. It was a charity event for the local animal shelter, the same event that Marcus was attending with Cinnamon. It was a worthy cause, and I'd been more than happy to be a small part of it when I'd accepted the offer. I had prepared four different crêpe batters ahead of time, as well as all the ingredients I would need to create my masterpieces. I would transport the food and prepare the crêpes at the location as they were ordered. Everything about the event appealed to me, except for the fact that I had to drive the delivery bike there.

I'd been nervous about it all day, but I kept telling myself that I could do it. As the exhaustion and frustration of the day caught up with me, I seriously doubted that I could pull it off. I was holding out hope that I could convince Tate to jump on his bike and go with me, but I hadn't actually asked him. Though if I knew Tate, he would do it in a heartbeat. He very rarely told me no.

"Hello, darling girl. I haven't seen you in days," Nellie called out to me as she stepped into the hallway and locked her apartment door behind her. "How are you doing?"

"Hey, Nellie. I'm doing all right," I lied. She didn't need to know that I was drowning in my own misery. I smiled and continued, "What are you up to?"

"I'm meeting a friend of mine for dinner," she answered with a smile.

"That's great. I'm so glad that you're getting out a bit more now. Do you have your cell phone with you? And your keys?" I was happy that she was heading out, but it would be dark soon, and Nellie was a bit too trusting. I worried about her safety.

"They're both right here in my handbag." The older woman patted her purse and nodded at me. "You're so sweet to worry."

"Of course I worry about you. You're my friend." I squeezed her arm tenderly.

"Are you and Tate doing anything special tonight?"

"I actually have to do a catering event across town later on. I have to ride the bike there. I'm hoping Tate will tag along with me."

"You're doing an event? On the bike?" Nellie's forehead wrinkled in concern. It hadn't taken her long to discover how accident-prone I was.

"Yes, unfortunately I am, Nellie. I can't back out of it now, and there's no one to do it but me." I shook my head and shrugged.

"I can't believe that horrible Melody left you in the lurch like that. You know, I saw her working at the grocery store around the corner the other day," Nellie said with a shake of her head.

"You did? I feel really sorry for her boss," I added.

"Well, I'm sure you'll be just fine. Do you have your cell phone with you?" Nellie smiled.

"Always. Now stop fussing over me and go enjoy your friend. I'll talk to you soon." I grinned at her, hugged her goodbye, and went inside my apartment.

Omelet decided she wanted to stay home that morning, so she greeted me at the door with a plaintive meow, announcing that it was dinnertime. I dropped my belongings in the foyer and followed her into the kitchen, where I prepared her food. Tate wasn't home yet, and I realized that he must be working a twenty-four-hour shift. Glancing at the calendar, I saw the date was blocked out in green, which meant he wouldn't be home until the following day.

My heart sank a little lower. I'd been counting on the fact that I could talk him into going with me. It might have been bearable then, and I wouldn't have been so worried about a possible disaster. It looked like I was on my own, so I figured I'd better pull up my big-girl pants and get on with it.

"Tell me I can do this, Omelet, because I'm having serious doubts." I glanced at my cat, but she refused to meet my eyes. Her refusal to look at me told me she had as little confidence in my biking abilities as I did.

Ignoring the voices in my head that said I was crazy even to attempt what I was about to do, I hooked Omelet's leash on her collar, headed to the storage room where I kept my bike, loaded up the food, and made my way out of the apartment building.

Once Omelet and I were on the sidewalk, I placed a pillow into the basket on the front of the bike and lifted her inside. I typed the address of the venue into the GPS on my phone, took a deep breath, and climbed on the bike. Omelet looked at me and squinted skeptically.

"Come on, how bad can it be? At the very least, I expect a little support from you," I scolded her. She tilted her head to the side and glared at me before finally settling herself onto her pillow.

I began pedaling down the sidewalk, trying to recall everything I'd ever learned about bicycling, which honestly wasn't much. I'd only done it a few times as a kid, and most of those incidents had ended in bloody knees, bruises, and one trip to the emergency room for a serious concussion.

I gave myself a pep talk as I continued on my route. *You're a grown woman now. It's just a bike. It has three wheels. You're literally riding a tricycle. Even toddlers can do that.*

After riding for several more blocks, I was surprised to admit that everything was going surprisingly well. I hadn't run over any pedestrians, all three wheels were still on the road, and everything was going according to plan. I congratulated myself on being a complete rock star—I was not only facing my fears, I was conquering them.

I turned the corner and rode a bit farther when I realized that somehow I had joined other people riding bikes, an entire herd of them to be exact. I didn't take an exact head count, but it was a very large group. What I estimated to be thousands of other bikers were crowded onto the street, and I had managed to end up smack-dab in the middle of them.

Normally it wouldn't be a big deal to be caught in the middle of a group of bikers. In this instance, however, I realized that I was more than a little bit overdressed for the occasion. Every single rider around me was stark naked!

At first, I thought that perhaps I was hallucinating, but the sheer amount of flesh surrounding me told me otherwise. The fact that I was fully clothed stuck out like a sore thumb. Somehow I had ended up in the middle of Portland's World Naked Bike Ride, a yearly event that protested fossil fuel dependency and promoted body positivity and bike safety. In theory, I approved of the event, but I never imagined that I would be a part of it in any way. If at all possible, I preferred not to show my birthday suit in public. It wasn't that I was a prude. It just wasn't my thing.

My mind turned over the possibilities of how to remedy the situation, but I felt stuck. As much as I wanted to escape the predicament, I had no idea how to break free from the mob. There were just too many bikers around, and there was nowhere else for me to go. *Maybe I should just go with the flow. I'm a free spirit. I need to embrace it!* Besides, it wasn't like anyone was going to notice me in the crowd of naked people, unless I was the only one who was wearing clothes.

Making my decision without another thought, I maneuvered my way to the side of the street, took a deep breath, stripped off my clothes completely, and threw them into my bag. Omelet's eyes widened with shock.

"Don't be such a goody-goody, Omelet. Everyone else is doing it. It's not a big deal, and if I'm going to be naked, so are you." I quickly removed her sweater and ignored the scathing look she threw at me.

Folding her sweater, I stuffed it into my bag with my belongings and climbed back on the seat. I started pedaling again before I could second-guess my decision. After only a few blocks, I realized why people usually wore clothes to ride bikes. My skin was sticking to the seat, and I knew extensive chafing was inevitable. Having no idea how long the route was, I prayed that I'd joined up on the tail end and it would all be over soon.

Riding along with the group of unclothed, peaceful protestors, I decided to give in and embrace the festive spirit surrounding the event. I waved at the crowd of onlookers as I rode down the street, honked my bicycle horn, and smiled widely. It was almost like being in a parade. Me and a few thousand of my new naked friends continued down the street. I was actually starting to enjoy myself, other than the sweaty seat and the skin irritation.

All at once I heard a fire siren, followed by the deafening sound of the truck's horn. The street lights abruptly turned red. The wailing sound continued as it grew closer. *Fire trucks equal Tate. Tate seeing me naked in public equals bad news.* I told myself that there were many fire trucks, and even more firefighters in Portland. What were the odds that Tate was in that particular truck?

Since the traffic light up ahead had turned red, half of the group went through the light, but the other half had to stop. I ended up in the front line of the group that was waiting for the traffic signal to change.

Glancing around, I noticed that the cars were all stopped at the intersecting streets. Needless to say, every single person inside of the stopped vehicles gawked at the spectacle in front of them. I really couldn't blame them. How often did one see thousands of naked people riding bicycles?

As I waited, a shiny, red fire truck sped through the intersection, and my heart sank in my chest when I spotted Tate riding in the front seat of the vehicle. I prayed that he wouldn't see me, but it was no use. His head whipped around in my direction as the truck flew by. When my eyes met his, there was no doubt that I had been spotted, and I knew I would have some serious explaining to do.

Before I could even think about that problem, my circumstances took an even bigger nosedive as I spotted the sleek black Mercedes stopped at the light adjacent to me. The window lowered slowly and my father's stern face peered out. He blinked twice and shook his head, as if he were trying to expel the image of his daughter sitting at a Portland stoplight, completely naked, on a bicycle. Elizabeth, my oh-so-perfect stepmother, leaned over from the passenger seat to get a closer look.

There wasn't much I could do, seeing as how I was sitting right next to them. With no apparent escape route, I did the only thing I could do—I smiled and waved.

"Hey, Dad. Hey, Elizabeth. I see you're back from London. Did you have a good time?"

My stepmother didn't answer the question, just continued to gawk.

"Willow Simpson, what in Heaven's name do you think you're doing?" I knew my poor father, the dictionary's definition of propriety, was baffled once again at the shenanigans of his bumbling daughter.

"Oh, I'm not doing much, Dad. I'm just out for a bike ride with a few of my friends." I felt my face flush even more, and I had no doubt that the rest of my skin was just as red as my hair.

"Where are your clothes?"

"Oh, don't worry, they're right here." I gestured toward the bag that was attached to the basket.

"Well, then perhaps you should put them on," Dad suggested through clenched teeth.

Elizabeth seemed to have recovered from the shock and burst into a fit of laughter. I was certain that she was going to have a heyday telling her friends at the country club all about her crazy stepdaughter's latest antics. Just then, I saw several bright flashes and realized that they were coming from the cameras of the photographers from the local media.

Of course, I was directly in their line of vision. Somehow I just knew that a picture of me, sitting stark naked on the Dancing Crêpe's delivery bike, would end up in the next edition of the newspaper.

I swear if I didn't have bad luck, I would have no luck at all.

Thankfully the light changed, and the crowd of bike riders began to move. As I pedaled away, I called behind me, "I'll talk to you soon, Dad. I have to get to work."

I rode another couple of blocks when the group slowly began to disperse. I realized we had reached the end of the Naked Bike route. Glancing at my GPS, I saw that my destination was only a block away. I waved goodbye to the group, pulled into the alley next to the benefit, and threw my clothes back on.

I had arrived without hurting anyone, although the amount of flesh I'd witnessed had certainly been an experience. All I had to do at that point was go into the benefit, cook some crêpes, and make it back home in one piece.

"We can do this, Omelet. Let's compose ourselves and get to work."

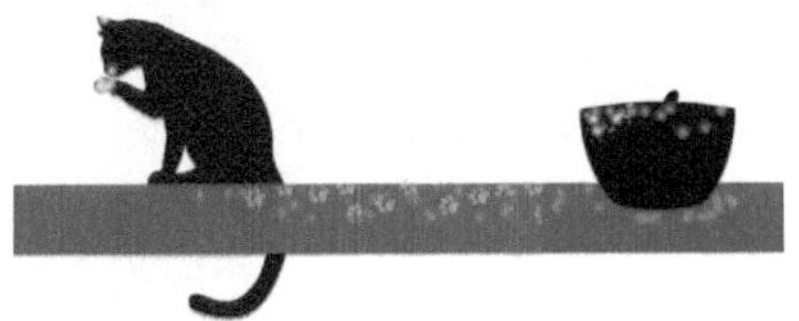

CHAPTER TEN

As usual, Tate had been a real trooper when I explained the reason why I was naked in downtown Portland the night of the bike ride fiasco. Of course, he told me that his firefighter friends had given him a hard time when they saw his fiancée, the exhibitionist. Although I wanted to protest, the fact remained that I did manage to lose my clothes at the most inopportune moments. There wasn't much I could say to refute it.

Even though Tate had quickly put the subject of my nudity to bed, Dad wasn't nearly as sympathetic to my plight. He had called me that very night and raked me over the coals about how embarrassed he was by my behavior. He gave me the whole song and dance routine, reminding me for the umpteenth time that I was a Simpson and I should conduct myself accordingly. It was the same lecture I'd been getting from him for as long as I could remember.

No matter how old I got, some things never changed, especially the fact that I always managed to disappoint my father. Surprisingly, Elizabeth called me right after that and said she thought my dad was overreacting. She then thanked me for giving her a good laugh. That woman never ceased to amaze me. Just when I thought I had her figured out, she threw something new my way.

Tate had arrived home from work early the following morning, and even though I told him that he needed to go to sleep, he insisted that he wanted to spend some time with me. Omelet made it clear that she wanted to stay home, so we left her napping in her favorite corner and headed out for the day.

Things had been so hectic lately that I hadn't even had time to entertain Suzanne with the gory details of the Melody saga. I was sure my favorite barista was chomping at the bit for all the gossip, and I missed talking to my friend, so Tate and I decided to stop by Simpson Coffee on our way to the Dancing Crêpe.

"Morning, Tate. Morning, Willow. One black coffee and one butterscotch latte with extra butterscotch coming right up," Suzanne called with a smile as we walked through the door.

"Thanks, Suzanne." I smiled at her as Tate grabbed the table nearest the counter so we could chat while she worked.

For once, we happened to be the only people in the coffee shop. I draped my bag over the back of the chair and leaned on the counter while she prepared our drinks, filling her in on all the joys of firing my first employee.

"I can't believe Melody lasted that long. How in the world did you avoid killing her?" Suzanne smirked at me as she handed Tate his coffee and got to work on my butterscotch latte. "Tate, you were way off on how long it would take Willow to fire that girl. You didn't give it more than a couple of days."

"Yeah, she held out a lot longer than I thought she

could. There were a few times when I was convinced that I'd have to bail her out of jail, though." Tate chuckled as he sipped his black coffee.

"All right, you two, give it a rest. I know I made a bad call with Melody, but I've taken care of it. I've learned my lesson. I will never again be hasty when hiring an employee." Rolling my eyes, I slumped into my chair and waited for Suzanne to finish making my drink.

"I told you not to hire a woman, Willow. I know you. Stick to hiring guys. That's the only way it's going to work out." Suzanne grinned and placed my latte in front of me.

Tate's forehead crinkled in distaste as he placed his coffee on the table and crossed his arms. "I disagree. I don't think Willow should hire a man."

"At least she shouldn't hire a cute one, right, Tate?" Suzanne teased with a wink.

"I couldn't care less about what a man looks like." Tate squirmed in his seat. I knew he didn't want to admit it, but Suzanne had hit the nail right on the head.

"Well, you two, I think I may have actually found someone. I've been scouring through the pile of applications I've received, and most of them got two gigantic thumbs down for one reason or another. There was one candidate who really stood out, though. I called and checked out both his personal and work references yesterday, and this guy got nothing but stellar recommendations from everyone I talked to. He's also worked jobs in food service, so I'm sure he knows his way around a kitchen." I grinned widely and inwardly crossed my fingers.

"He? It's a man?" Tate cleared his throat and tried not to look alarmed, but his displeasure was written all over his handsome face.

"Yes, it's a man. His name is Wyatt Miller. He's

supposed to stop by the Dancing Crêpe sometime today so I can meet him. From everything I've heard, I'm sure I'm going to like him." I smiled and guzzled some more of my drink.

"Let's just hope she doesn't like him too much, right, Tate?" Suzanne giggled as she jokingly punched Tate in the arm. She really got a kick out of trying to rile my fiancé.

"That's not going to be a problem, because there's no other guy for me except this one." I leaned across the small table and planted a big kiss on Tate's cheek as we both stood to leave.

"C'mon, Tate, you know I'm just giving you a hard time. Willow is crazy for you. You've got nothing to worry about." Suzanne returned to stand behind the front counter. "Besides, if Marcus Tucker couldn't steal her from you, then it simply cannot be done, because that man is *hot*." She rolled her eyes and fanned herself for effect.

"You think Marcus Tucker is hot? Well, let me know if you need me to douse those flames for you, Suzanne. I wouldn't want you to burn up." Tate grinned and draped his arm around my shoulder.

"We should be going. I want to make sure everything is running smoothly before Wyatt stops by." I grabbed my drink, my purse, and Tate's hand.

"Keep me posted," Suzanne called as we exited.

"You know I will," I returned as the door shut behind me.

Tate and I hopped on the MAX, and it wasn't long before we arrived at the Dancing Crêpe. Since he knew the opening routine nearly as well as I did, he jumped in and helped me get the truck prepared for the day. We worked side by side, completely comfortable and perfectly in sync. Our rhythm was natural, and Tate was like an extension of me. Suzanne was right; he had nothing to worry about. My heart was his.

I knew my amazing guy needed to go home and get some sleep, but he wanted to spend some extra time with me before he took off. Our schedules were so hectic that we didn't get nearly enough hours to just hang out with one another. He was always trying to do everything within his power to make me happy. I had hit the fiancé jackpot with that one. Hopefully, if Wyatt worked out as an employee, I might be able to take a day off once in a while and do some nice things for Tate in return.

Flipping the sign to Open, I smiled as the line began to form. I could already tell that it was going to be a busy morning, and although I was tired, I was also grateful. Those customers were the lifeblood of my business, and I needed them to keep coming back for more. Amazingly, they did, and my lines grew longer every single day.

Tate and I worked quickly through the rush, and I was glad that he'd decided to spend the morning in the truck with me. Some days it was so busy that I could barely keep up. I really hoped the new employee thing worked out.

"Excuse me, are you Willow?"

I glanced out the window and smiled at the man standing there. About six feet tall, his body long, lean, and wiry, he had the look of a runner. His chestnut brown hair was shaggy in a rumpled, sexy way, and his blue eyes sparkled with mischief. He smiled widely, and I noticed that his teeth were just the slightest bit crooked, but that little imperfection only added to the charm of the total package. He'd spoken only five words, but his very presence commanded attention; he was practically dripping with charm and charisma.

"Yes... I'm Willow," I replied.

Tate leaned in next to me and eyed the man in front of us. He didn't look at all pleased. "And I'm going to take a shot in the dark and say you must be Wyatt."

The man extended his hand to Tate. "Yeah, I'm Wyatt. Wyatt Miller. How did you know?"

"Wild guess," Tate said quietly as he returned the handshake.

I extended my hand to Wyatt and repeated the gesture. I had an entire speech prepared, but at the moment, I couldn't remember any of it. I realized that I'd been shaking Wyatt's hand far longer than was necessary, and I told myself to pull it together and act professionally. Handsome, charming, charismatic Wyatt wasn't at all what I'd expected him to be, and he'd caught me totally off guard.

If he works out, maybe I can introduce him to Suzanne.

"Why don't you come inside? We can chat in here." I cleared off the chair inside the food truck so Wyatt would have a place to sit.

He stepped through the door and took the seat as I gestured toward it. The small space suddenly felt quite cramped with all three of us in there. Tate leaned on the counter, trying to appear casual, but I could tell he was uptight about the situation.

I was much more nervous than I'd anticipated. I had pictured Wyatt as a common, everyday, average-looking dude, which he so obviously was not. *Just play it cool, Willow. Act natural. The fact that he's cute will be good for business.* I took a deep breath and jumped right into the conversation I had rehearsed in my mind the night before.

"So, Wyatt, I've checked out all your references, and I have to say that everyone spoke very highly of you. It sounds to me like you're a hard worker, and as a bonus, you've also had some food service experience. Tell me about that." I was proud of myself for sounding so polished, even though I was more than a little bit nervous to be meeting my potential new employee.

"Yes, I grew up working in my grandparents' diner in Ohio. I know how to cook everything on their menu, and I'm pretty comfortable in a kitchen. I know all about taking orders and filling them, and I'm quick and friendly." Wyatt smiled widely, and two perfect dimples indented his cheeks. He was painfully adorable.

"It says on your application that you only moved to Portland recently. What brought you all the way out here from Ohio?" I glanced at the paperwork I held in my hand, although I had basically memorized his stats already.

"I'm a musician. I hooked up online with a group of guys from Portland, and we formed a band. That's easier to pull off when you're all in the same state." He chuckled loudly. It sounded like music.

"You're a musician? What do you play?" Musicians had been my Achilles heel for as long as I could remember. On top of his musical abilities, he had personality in spades.

It's no wonder that Tate doesn't like him.

"Oh, I can play pretty much anything. And I sing. I'm really hoping the band thing takes off, but in the meantime, I need a steady job."

"So you're only looking for something temporary? Well, that might be a deal breaker, Wyatt. I'm pretty sure Willow wants an employee who's going to stick around for a while. It would be a waste of her time to train someone who just turns around and leaves when something better comes along." Tate raised his eyebrows at Wyatt.

"If I get the job, I don't plan to leave any time soon. I'm very loyal. Besides, most of the band's gigs are at night, so there shouldn't be any conflicts. I'm a dependable guy."

Wyatt shifted uncomfortably in his chair and smiled at Tate, who didn't return the nicety.

"I do have to say, Wyatt, that dependable was a word that came up more than once when I called your references." Every single person I called had done nothing but sing his praises. "Out of curiosity, which venues have your band played?"

"At this point, we play any gig we can get. So far, it's been mostly bars, clubs, weddings, and one Bar Mitzvah. We even had an offer to play at a strip club, but the timing didn't work out," Wyatt chuckled.

"Was it the vegan strip club?" I asked.

"Portland has a vegan strip club?" Wyatt's face registered shock.

"Of course Portland has a vegan strip club. I know the chef there. He tells me it's a real meat market." I grinned at him. "You see what I did there?"

"That's a good one." Wyatt smiled.

He seemed to get my quirky sense of humor, which was a good sign. My gut told me that I had all the information I needed in order to make my decision, but if hiring Melody had taught me anything, it was that I needed to take my time.

"Wyatt, I'll be honest with you. I was hoping that maybe you would spend the afternoon working in the truck with me to see what the job is all about. I just want to make sure that hiring you will be a good fit for the both of us. After that, we'll know better if it's going to work out or not. Does that sound agreeable to you?"

"It sure does! I'd love to try it out. And I just have to say that I think your food truck has the most creative names and menu that I've ever seen. I have a feeling we're going to work really well together, Willow." Wyatt grinned.

Those darn dimples are not winning him any points with Tate.

"Perfect," I replied as I shook his hand.

Tate glanced at his watch and grimaced. I knew he needed to go home and sleep, and I also knew that was the last thing he wanted to do at that moment. I felt bad that he didn't like Wyatt, but there was little I could do about it. My intuition told me he was going to be the perfect employee.

"I have to run. I hope it works out for you, Wyatt." Tate's face didn't mirror his words. He nodded curtly, grabbed his bag, and walked outside. I followed. Once we were out of earshot, Tate made his opinion known.

"Willow, it sounds to me like he's too good to be true. I'll bet his references were just making all that stuff up." Tate raised one eyebrow suspiciously. "What do you think? You aren't buying his good-guy routine, are you?"

"I don't know, Tate. He seemed pretty genuine to me. Let's just see how the afternoon goes. I won't make any decisions until I find out how well we can work together." I hugged him tightly and could feel the tension in his body. He always worried so much.

"It's your decision, of course. Just don't be sucked in by his pretty face. And you know as well as I do that you've always had a thing for musicians. Remember Justin Wills in high school? He played his guitar for you one time, and you were like putty in his hands." Tate ran his hands through his hair in frustration.

"I'm not a teenager anymore, Tate. And besides, in case you haven't noticed, I have a thing for firemen these days." I stood on my tiptoes and wrapped my arms around him, drawing his face close to mine. I pressed my lips against his and kissed him deeply, hoping to reassure him that he had nothing to worry about.

"I'm going to hold you to that. Just make sure that if you hire him, you tell him to leave his guitar at home."

"I'll let you know how it goes tonight. Love you," I said as I squeezed his hand.

"Love you too, babe."

Omelet and I ran quickly from the bus stop toward the Dancing Crêpe. The sky had opened up in a deluge that morning, and the sidewalk looked more like a small lake than concrete. The rain pelted down on my hood and ran like a waterfall off Omelet's purple rain jacket. We splashed through a giant puddle, and I was glad that I'd made Omelet wear her red rain boots. She hated having wet paws almost as much as she hated it when I skimped on her tuna serving at dinnertime.

Arriving at the food truck, I noticed that the lights were already on. Wyatt must have come in early again. He'd been working for me for three weeks, and hiring that man was truly one of the best business decisions I'd ever made. He was a natural with the customers and everyone loved him.

He was fast, friendly, and dependable, had immediately picked up on the routine, and he could already prepare every crêpe on the menu nearly as well as I could. Best of all, he came in early every morning and had almost all the prep work completed by the time I arrived. He was also a whiz as a bike delivery guy, managing to double the number of orders I could send out in a day. He was truly the dream employee I'd been waiting for.

The only downside was that Tate wasn't Wyatt's biggest fan. As much as my guy liked to deny it, I knew his opinion had nothing at all to do with my new employee's work ethic. The truth was that my fiancé was jealous, plain and simple, and it wasn't hard to understand why. Wyatt was the kind of guy women loved, and men loved to hate.

Wyatt and I got along with one another like we had been friends for years, rather than just a few weeks. We worked well together, and within a few days, we could finish each other's sentences. We had the same strange sense of humor, and he had the artistic, creative energy I loved being around. He was constantly cracking jokes, and he made our work environment extra enjoyable. There was never a dull moment with Wyatt around.

He sang songs all day long, and although I'd promised Tate that Wyatt wouldn't bring his guitar to work, I hadn't exactly followed through with banning it. I couldn't help it. Wyatt used me as a sounding board for his new music, and his songs were fantastic. There was no way I was going to tell him to stop. The customers loved his music too, and he'd taken to practicing outside during our downtime. His voice was like honey, and people flocked in because of it. His music was good for my business, and so was he.

"Morning, Wyatt. How long have you been here?" I greeted him as Omelet and I entered.

I stripped off my rain jacket, then removed hers as well, hanging them both to dry. She trotted to her bed in the corner and began her morning grooming session.

"Oh, I've been here about an hour or so. You know I'm an early morning guy. I like coming in while it's still dark and quiet. I get some of my best ideas for songs then." He grinned as he whipped up the sweet buttermilk crêpe batter.

"You know I'm not going to complain about it, even though I can't imagine wanting to wake up any earlier than I have to in the morning. Tate usually has to drag me out of bed kicking and screaming. Even after all these years of getting up early, I still hate it." I washed my hands and began working beside him.

"You should take a morning off one of these days, once you trust me to handle things." Wyatt grinned, and those pesky little dimples of his had me smiling right back at him.

"Honestly, I trust you to handle things already. You don't know how amazing I think you are. As a matter of fact, I was just bragging about you to Tate last night."

"That's probably why he hates me," he chuckled softly.

"He doesn't hate you... exactly," I hedged.

"Your fiancé doesn't like me, and we all know it. It's all right. I get it. If you were my girl, I wouldn't want you spending so much time in a cramped space with another guy." Wyatt shrugged, poured the batter into the storage container, and placed it in the refrigerator.

"Tate's just a little overprotective. Don't take it personally. He'll come around, especially if having you here gives me the ability to take a day off every once in a while." I smiled.

"Well, like I said, I'm game for giving you a break whenever you're ready." Wyatt glanced at the clock and turned on the Open sign. I looked outside and noticed the line was already forming for the day.

We worked side by side for the next few hours. After the lunch rush died down, Wyatt ran across the street to retrieve the delivery bike from the storage unit I'd rented. It didn't make sense to keep the bike at my apartment when we needed it close to the food truck each day, so I'd done some checking and found that I could store it right across the street. It was the perfect solution.

When he returned, I gave Wyatt the delivery list for the day. He loaded up the trailer, waved goodbye, and took off. I knew he would do exactly what I'd asked him to, and if there were any problems, he would deal with them. Having a trustworthy employee was a huge weight off my shoulders. The differences between Melody and Wyatt were like night and day.

The rain had stopped by that point, and the sun was peeking through the clouds. Omelet was napping in her box, so I decided to take a towel outside to dry off my outdoor seating area while there was a bit of a lull in the activity.

I had just finished drying the chairs when I sensed someone watching me. Turning around, I had to grip the edge of the chair in order to avoid falling over. Standing on the sidewalk was a woman who looked almost exactly like me.

She had frizzy, wild red curls that were the same color as my own. Her hazel eyes mirrored mine precisely. The only difference was the slightest beginning of fine lines around hers. Her porcelain skin was identical to mine, and the smattering of freckles on her face was like looking at my own in a mirror. Our slender bodies were even shaped the same, although I noticed that she was far too thin. She was dressed in a flowy flowered peasant dress and the oldest pair of Birkenstocks I had ever seen. Besides the fact that she was very dirty and unkempt, the woman could have been me in twenty years.

"You must be Willow." She smiled and moved slowly toward me.

"Who... what... how do you know my name?" I stammered, swallowing hard and trying not to pass out.

"You are the spitting image of your mother. I would know you anywhere." She spoke quietly as she stood within arm's reach of me.

"How do you know my mother?" My brain was racing a million miles an hour, trying to make sense of the doppelgänger. "Who are you?"

"I'm Juniper Rain Tremaine. Fern, your mama, was my older sister." Her already pale skin blanched to an even lighter shade, and I knew I wasn't the only one who was spooked by the encounter.

"You're my aunt? Are you sure? I suppose that's a silly question. Of course you are. You look just like me, and you look exactly like the picture I have of Mama." I had no idea what I was supposed to do with this shocking information. I didn't even know my mother had a younger sister. I was under the impression that everyone in her family was gone.

"I'm sure this is a surprise, Willow, and I'm sorry it's taken me so long to talk to you. I've spent a good while working myself up to it." Juniper plopped onto the bench beside me, and I collapsed into the chair that I'd been drying a few moments before.

"What do you mean, it took you a long time? How long have you known about me?"

"Oh, honey, I've known about you since you were born. Our parents died after Fern left for Portland, and I was just a wee thing. I lived in the commune with another family. They were good to me. Your mama wanted me to come live with her, but she was so young herself, and she had you to take care of. And then she got sick. It was better for everyone if I just stayed where I was. I always wanted to meet you someday, though." Juniper picked at her dirty fingernails. She kept darting her eyes away from mine, almost as if it was hard for her to look at me for too long.

"So you just arrived in Portland, then?" I was working hard to wrap my brain around all the new information.

"No, I've been here for several years." Juniper fidgeted in her seat and smoothed the worn fabric of her dirty dress.

"Several years? And you're just now telling me who you are? I don't understand. Why didn't you find me sooner?"

"It's complicated." Juniper's eyes finally met mine, and the eerie connection I felt with her made my head spin.

"It can't be all that complicated. Where do you live? What do you do?"

"That's the complicated part. You see, I don't really live anywhere." As she spoke, her eyes once again left mine, and she sat there staring at her lap.

"You're... homeless?" I practically whispered the word.

It wasn't as if I didn't know anyone who was homeless. I lived in Portland, after all. I just couldn't imagine one of my own family members being homeless, not when I'd grown up in a mansion. The injustice of it all caused my stomach to churn.

"Oh, it's not really as bad as it sounds." She shrugged and continued to avoid my gaze. It suddenly made sense why she'd been embarrassed to introduce herself to me, the daughter of one of the richest men in the world.

"I imagine that living on the streets isn't very pleasant, Juniper. But I still don't understand why you waited so long to tell me you were here. I could have helped you." I tentatively reached out and took her hand in my own. It was icy cold.

"Barringer Simpson's wealth was no secret. Everybody back home knew Fern had married into one of the richest families in the country. I knew you were well taken care of, and I never wanted to interfere. Besides, I wasn't sure how my presence would be received by a man like your father. I figured that if your homeless, hippie aunt showed up, neither you nor your father would be too interested. But finally, I convinced myself that you were a grown woman and could make up your own mind about me. Like I said, it took me a long time to work up the nerve." Juniper squeezed my hand, and my heart constricted.

She was the only connection I had to my mother, and even though believing the story of a complete stranger sounded crazy, I wasn't about to turn her away. Besides, I knew without a doubt that she was telling me the truth. She was a part of me; I could feel it when she looked at me. I thought about all the years that I'd spent longing for my mom, and meeting her sister seemed like a gift that was too good to be true.

"I'm really glad you found me. I just wish you'd done it sooner." I rose to my feet and she followed suit. "I don't mean to pry, but when was the last time you had a good meal, Juniper?"

"Oh, it hasn't been too long. Only a couple of days or so." She shrugged and raised her head proudly.

"Come with me. One thing you'll figure out pretty quickly is that when I don't know what to do, I cook. Let me fix you a crêpe." I grabbed my aunt's hand and led her into the food truck.

"That sounds delicious," she replied as she followed me.

"Oh, and you can kiss your life on the streets goodbye. You're coming home with me tonight."

"That's not what I came here for. I don't want a hand-out." Juniper stopped walking and crossed her arms defiantly. It was like looking at me when I threw one of my hissy fits with Tate.

"This isn't a handout. I'll expect you to earn your keep. I'll help you find a job. You can help me in a hundred different ways. That's what families do for each other, Juniper." I took a deep breath and pulled her into my arms, hugging the familiar stranger tightly.

It only took a couple of seconds before I felt her relax and she threw her arms around me as well. Her body shook with sobs. I got the distinct feeling that she'd been holding in those tears for a lot of years.

I had no idea what I was doing, and if someone had told me that morning that I would be bringing a homeless woman to my apartment that night, I would have laughed at the ridiculousness of it. In my gut, though, I knew I was doing the right thing.

No matter the outcome, finding out that my mother's sister existed and could possibly become a part of my life made me happy in a way that I'd never imagined.

Now I just had to figure out how to explain it all to Tate and Omelet.

CHAPTER TWELVE

I snuggled closer to Tate as I glanced at the clock on the bedside table. It was Saturday morning, and normally the alarm would have awakened us hours ago. Thankfully, Wyatt was taking the early morning shift by himself so Tate and I could have some much-needed alone time. I was hoping that if Wyatt could provide us with more time together, it would make Tate like my new friend a little bit more, but I wasn't holding my breath.

Tate's eyes were closed and his body was warm. His breathing was slow and steady, and I propped my head on my arm and watched him sleep. My heart constricted a bit as I thought about our emotional conversation the night before. *The way you reacted was certainly not one of your finest moments, Willow. You have every reason to feel guilty.* As usual, I had managed to create a mess of everything.

Before bed, Tate had started talking about the wedding again, and he'd pressed me to set a date. Like a deer caught in the headlights, I panicked. I didn't mean to sound defensive when I told him I wasn't ready, but looking back on it, I knew that was exactly how it had come out. I suppose it probably had something to do with the fact that I burst into tears and yelled, "Have you lost your mind? I can't do it!"

Tate wanted to get married in the fall. He'd made it clear all along that he was ready to tie the knot as soon as possible, but it all started to implode the night before when Tate grabbed the calendar and circled the date in red. I became incredibly stressed out when I realized it was only three months away.

He'd told me a while ago that he wanted an October wedding, and at the time it had seemed somewhere in the distant future. So like any good fiancée, I'd nodded and absentmindedly agreed.

Big mistake.

As the months began to fly by, I'd kept pushing the marriage conversation to the back burner. Every time Tate brought up our wedding plans, I changed the subject. It wasn't that I didn't want to marry him specifically. The problem was that I didn't want to marry anyone.

Nellie kept telling me it was just cold feet, but I wasn't so sure. What if it was more than that? I'd agreed to the engagement because I loved Tate, and if I could possibly imagine married life with anyone, it was him. As the ideas became more concrete, though, and talk of actual wedding plans began, I found myself balking.

The concept of settling down terrified me. All I could think of was Dad and his string of wives. The idea wasn't appealing to me. If I ever got married, that was that; I was only doing it once, so it had better be right. It was easier to just avoid doing it at all than to do it and get it wrong.

I didn't want to hurt Tate, but that's exactly what I had done when I'd freaked out and told him I couldn't get married in October. I'd given him the excuse that it wasn't possible to plan a wedding that quickly, but we both knew that wasn't true. Neither of us wanted a big event, and we could have easily pulled off a small wedding in that amount of time.

He said we could go to the courthouse for all he cared. He just wanted us to be married. The mere thought of actually tying the knot made me break out in a cold sweat.

Why can't I just be a normal fiancée and plan a stupid wedding?

I loved Tate more than I had ever loved another human being. I didn't want to be with anyone but him, and I didn't want him to go anywhere. Marriage would change everything. It was inevitable. I had no idea what to do or how to fix the dilemma, but time was ticking, and I needed to figure it out. I had to either jump ship or get fully on board. Tate didn't deserve anything less.

His green eyes opened, and he smiled when he saw me looking at him. "Morning, babe."

"Good morning," I replied as I scooted closer to him. "It was nice not waking up to an alarm for a change, wasn't it?"

"It sure was. Too bad we can't do this every morning." He shifted and wrapped his arms around me, nuzzling my neck softly before planting a kiss there.

"Tate, about last night...," I began.

"Forget it. I'm sorry I pushed you." He rubbed his hands rhythmically up and down my back.

"Don't you dare apologize. I'm the one who freaked out and lost my mind. You know I love you. Tell me you know it." I rolled over and pushed my back against his chest, snuggling in close to him. His arms engulfed me, and I felt safe and cherished.

"I do know you love me, babe. And I also know you'll marry me eventually. I really don't mean to rush you. I know you're scared. I just want to be your husband." He caressed the length of my body.

"You're too good to me. I don't know how you put up with me."

That was the deep dark truth of it. No matter what Tate said, I knew I wasn't nearly good enough for a man like him. I didn't deserve his selfless, unconditional love. My worst fear was that eventually, he would see that, too. Then he would leave me.

Tate moved his body and maneuvered me so I was lying flat on my back. He leaned over and locked his eyes on mine. "Enough. We'll talk more about it when you're ready. I'm happy to have you in any way I can."

I reached up and pulled his face toward mine, hungrily tasting his sweet lips. "I love you so much more than you will ever know," I whispered between kisses as I pulled his body closer.

Just when things were about to get really exciting, we heard a knock on the bedroom door.

"Willow, I'm sorry to bother you, but can I take a shower? Remember I have that job interview today." The sound of Juniper's voice was muffled through the door.

"Sure, Aunt June. Just give us a minute," I answered with a sigh and a roll of my eyes.

"Guess that means we're going to have to take a rain check on our fun, huh?" Tate said as he rolled out of bed and threw on pants and a T-shirt.

"I'm so sorry. We just can't catch a break, can we?" I jumped out of bed and quickly threw on my clothes.

"It's all right. I think what you're doing for Juniper is pretty wonderful. I really like her, you know."

"I can't believe she's been here for two weeks already. She's great, isn't she? I really hope this interview goes well for her today. She needs a fresh start." I unlocked the bedroom door, and Tate and I went into the kitchen while Juniper headed into the bathroom to get ready for her big day.

When I brought her home that first night, I was worried that Tate would think I was insane for doing so. As soon as he saw her, though, he seemed to know as well as I did that she was a part of me. He'd welcomed her with open arms and had asked very few questions. They got along well, even though he secretly told me that it was a bit eerie that she looked so much like me. I had to agree with him.

She'd been sleeping in my tiny spare bedroom, and the arrangement was fine, other than the fact that I only had one bathroom, which happened to be in my bedroom. There were times, like that morning, when it was a little inconvenient, but I wasn't about to let her go back to living on the streets.

She helped out around the house, and although she was a terrible cook, she was an excellent cleaner. Omelet loved Juniper because she gave her extra snacks, and for the first time in my life, I was getting a little taste of what it might have been like to have a mother. Juniper fussed over me, and she seemed to get great joy out of taking care of me.

I found out that Juniper had been a yoga instructor, but it had been several years since she had taught. I happened to have a customer who owned a yoga studio, and I'd pulled a few strings to get Juniper an interview. If it all went well, it would be the first job she'd had in many years. I knew she was nervous, and I hoped against hope that it worked out for her. She needed to feel like a productive citizen again.

Tate and I ate breakfast in silence, each of us lost in our own thoughts. When he finished eating, he grabbed his bag, kissed me goodbye, and headed off to work with the promise of picking up where we'd left off as soon as we had the chance.

Once Juniper was ready, I hugged Omelet goodbye and accompanied my aunt to her job interview. My stomach churned nervously as I waited for her, but I knew it had gone well as soon as she came out. She was beaming, and her eyes twinkled in a way that I hadn't seen since I'd met her.

"Well, how did it go? Did you get the job, June?" I asked her excitedly.

"Oh, Willow, it was wonderful. They loved me. I start work tomorrow, and I'll be on the schedule with my own classes by next week!" She hugged me and gave me a quick kiss on the cheek.

We went out to lunch at my favorite French bistro, Bonjour, to celebrate.

"I bought something for you, Aunt June," I said as we waited for our lunch.

"You don't need to buy me anything. You've already done enough, Willow," she said with a shake of her head.

"It's not a big deal. They're things you're going to need." I handed her the package.

Juniper's eyes filled with tears as she opened the box and looked inside. "You are too good to me."

"I love having you around. Besides, you're going to need the bus pass, and unless you plan to teach in your dresses, you'll need the yoga clothes." I smiled, certain my mom would have been happy that we'd found one another.

After finishing our meal, Juniper used her new bus pass, and Omelet and I headed to the Dancing Crêpe. I realized I hadn't been a bit worried about leaving the food truck in Wyatt's capable hands for nearly the whole day. When we arrived, everything was running like clockwork. I smiled to myself, thinking my life was pretty amazing. Everything was going exactly as planned.

"Well, it looks like you've got everything under control here. Thanks for the break." I grinned as I washed my hands and began filling orders.

"It was my pleasure. You'll be happy to know that it's been a busy day so far. If you're good here, I'll go ahead and make that delivery now." Wyatt grabbed the box that he'd already prepared. He'd also brought the bike over from the storage building already. The man was like a machine!

"You know, Wyatt, there's only this one delivery today, and it's just down the road. You've been working all morning. Would you like me to take it?"

For the safety of everyone involved, I normally didn't make the deliveries, but I felt like I'd already asked a lot of him that day. I didn't want him to get burned out and quit. At that point, I didn't know how I would get along without him. I had come to depend upon him more than I thought I would.

"I know how much you hate the deliveries, Willow. Really, I don't mind." He smiled at me.

"No, it's totally fine. It won't hurt me to do a delivery every now and then. Omelet can come with me," I replied as I grabbed the box. "I'll be right back."

Omelet trotted behind me and jumped into the basket as I loaded the order into the trailer. I climbed on the bike and pedaled down the street. The destination was only two blocks away. I could be there and back in a matter of minutes. *Easy peasy.*

I hummed along in the bike lane and came to a stop as the traffic light in front of me turned red. I felt my phone vibrate in my pocket, so I pulled it out and answered a text from Dad. He wanted to know if Tate and I would come over for dinner the next weekend. I hadn't seen him since the mishap during the Naked Bike Ride, and while I wasn't too eager to relive the moment with him and Elizabeth, I knew I should accept. I replied with a quick **Sure thing.**

"Not my favorite activity, but I'm trying to be a good daughter, Omelet," I said as I glanced up from my phone.

I felt myself falling into a downward spiral, and my heart constricted in my chest when I realized that Omelet was no longer in the basket. I'd only glanced away for a second, but she was gone.

CHAPTER THIRTEEN

Somehow I managed to maneuver myself out of the bike lane and onto the sidewalk. Frantically, I called Omelet's name as I looked desperately in each direction, hoping she was just playing a trick on me. *I only looked away for a second. Oh, Omelet, baby, where are you?*

I tried to catch my breath. I was practically hyperventilating, and I knew I had to pull myself together. *Think, Willow, think. Where could she have gone?* Maybe she was hiding from me. Maybe she thought it would be funny to scare me. *No, this feels different.* I wasn't sure why, but I knew without question that she'd been taken. Omelet stuck to my side like glue when we were out in public—unless there were cat treats involved. Had someone lured her from the basket with a snack?

My mind raced with a million thoughts, and each one sent me down an even darker path. Since I seemed to be having a panic attack, I couldn't slow them down. The horrible images inside of my brain continued to gain momentum. I had no idea what I should do. *Should I call the police? Could I file a report for a missing person?* Technically, Omelet wasn't a person, but she was my baby and she was missing! Some horrible monster had catnapped my Omelet, and I had to do something.

I needed to call Tate. And then I could call Marcus. He was a cop, so he would know what to do.

I was a blubbering mess. The people passing by on the sidewalk probably thought I was having some sort of mental episode, and they wouldn't be far from the truth. I had never felt such intense helplessness and panic, not even when I had been attacked myself. I just couldn't bear the thought of someone hurting Omelet.

At that moment, I didn't care what anyone thought of me. I grabbed my phone and dialed Tate's number.

"She's gone. Oh, Tate, Omelet's gone," I wailed as soon as he answered the phone.

"What do you mean she's gone? Slow down and tell me what's happening."

"She was in the basket and then she wasn't. I looked at my phone for one second and she was gone." I gulped air and hiccupped as I tried to breathe.

"Oh, babe, I'm so sorry. I'm going to take care of this. Tell me exactly where you are, and I'll call Marcus. He's a cop. He'll know what to do."

"Marcus? Why can't you come?"

"Babe, I wish I could. I'm at work and I can't leave. Believe me, I'd be there in a second if I could be. Just breathe with me. C'mon, babe."

Hearing Tate's soothing voice was just what I needed, and as I focused on my breathing, I began to calm down. I knew I had to keep myself on an even keel if I wanted to find Omelet. I had to be ready to give any information I knew to Marcus when he arrived. I rattled off the address to

Tate, who apologized again for not being able to drop every-thing and run to my rescue.

"It's okay. I know you can't leave work every time I'm having a crisis, which unfortunately seems to be often. Marcus will come. He'll be able to do something, right?" My voice quivered with emotion, but I breathed deeply and tried not to make Tate feel any worse than he did already.

"Listen to me. We will find her. If we have to walk the streets every single day looking for her, we will find Omelet, babe. Just focus on that."

"I hope you're right. I don't know what I'll do without her." Tears coursed down my cheeks, and I wiped them away with my sleeve. I needed to keep it together, but I couldn't seem to.

"I'm going to hang up now and call Marcus. He'll help you. You stay right there in case Omelet comes back," Tate instructed. "I love you."

"I love you, too."

I hung up the phone and attempted to get my emotions in check, trying not to think of the fact that Omelet was alone somewhere, or worse, being held hostage by someone with evil intentions. I had no idea how something so horrible could happen. How could she be with me one second and gone the next? How could someone take her and get away quickly enough for me to have missed it? Who would want to hurt my cat?

Maybe the better question is who wants to hurt me by taking her?

Not even five minutes later, a police patrol car pulled up to the sidewalk where I was sitting. Marcus jumped out, and the moment I saw his familiar face, I raced into his arms and threw myself at him. The tears started all over again.

"Hey, Tate just called and told me where you were. I

was patrolling in the area, so I came right over." Marcus hugged me tightly, and then he pulled a handkerchief from the pocket of his uniform and wiped my face. "Come on, tell me what happened."

"I don't know what happened," I wailed helplessly. "All I know is that she was here one second, and then she wasn't." My voice shook as I tried to turn off the water-works. "She's a good girl, but you know as well as I do that she'll make a break for it if someone offers her a treat. Someone bribed her to go with them, Marcus. What do I do?"

"I'm going to drive you home, and then we can come up with a game plan. Right now, we need to get you off the sidewalk." Marcus rubbed my back soothingly. "You're hysterical."

"What about my bike? I can't just leave it here." I ran my hands through my hair in frustration. Only a few minutes ago, everything in my life had seemed like it was humming along in the right direction. Now it was like a runaway train that had jumped the tracks.

"Is Wyatt working today?" Marcus tipped my face up toward his and forced me to look him in the eyes. I knew he was trying to get me to focus on what I needed to do next.

"Yes, I should call and let him know what happened." I grabbed my phone and dialed Wyatt's number.

He answered on the first ring, and as soon as I explained what was going on, he said he would lock up the food truck and be right there. He told me he would handle everything at the Dancing Crêpe for as long as I needed him to, and I thanked my lucky stars once again for hiring that man.

When he arrived only a few minutes later, he hugged me tightly, and I began sobbing once again. I was an emotional wreck.

"Willow, I'm so sorry about Omelet. I love that little girl." He patted my back.

"Thanks, Wyatt. I'm just so scared for her." My hands trembled as I fidgeted with the strap of my purse.

"Listen, don't worry about anything at work. I'm going to take care of it. I'll finish up the delivery, and then I'll stick around until closing time." He hopped on the bike. "I'm also going to make a zillion posters to hang up in the area. We're going to find her, Willow."

By the time I finally climbed into Marcus's patrol car, I felt like a dishrag that had been wrung out one too many times. I dissolved into a puddle of tears in the back seat. As we rode across town, I replayed the incident over and over again in my mind. It had all happened so quickly. The entire event felt like a blur.

Closing my eyes, I tried to slow my thoughts and focus on the details. I made myself remember the moment I looked away to return the text to Dad.

As I pictured it happening once again, I remembered something. At the time, it hadn't seemed important, but I knew every single detail might help. I closed my eyes and saw the tall woman running down the sidewalk, shouldering forcefully past the people strolling along. She had been wearing a hat and a long dark coat. Her wardrobe had struck me as odd, given the fact that the day was far too warm for a hat and coat.

I let myself sink even further inside the memory, and I remembered that the mystery woman had been carrying an oversized bag. It was deep and very large—the perfect size for holding a cat.

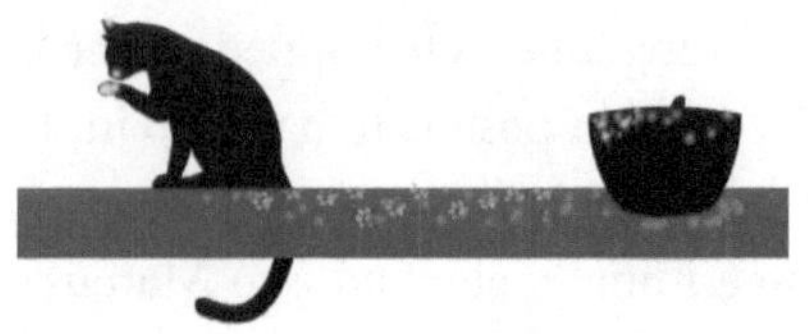

CHAPTER FOURTEEN

Marcus and I arrived back at my apartment within a few minutes. Walking through the front door without Omelet was one of the most gut-wrenching moments of my life. I started crying all over again when I spotted her cat bed in the corner of the living room and her food dishes in the kitchen. It was almost her dinnertime, and I wondered if she was hungry. Would the person who took her know how much she loved tuna? Would he or she even care?

I realized as soon as I was inside my front door that Tate had already called Juniper, because she met me there and pulled me into her arms. "Oh, honey, don't you worry. We're going to find that little girl. Look, I've already started making posters." Juniper gestured toward the kitchen table where the art supplies were scattered.

"Thanks, Aunt June. I just don't quite know what to do without her, you know? This all feels like a bad dream that I keep hoping I'll wake up from soon." I collapsed onto the sofa and hugged Omelet's favorite stuffed animal to my chest.

"Willow, honey, Tate just called and told me the news. I've brought you some raspberry scones." Nellie hurried in the front door and placed the tin of scones on the kitchen table before joining me on the sofa. "I'm here for you. Just tell me what you need." She hugged me tightly, and I placed my weary head on her comforting shoulder.

"It looks like you're in very good hands. I have to get back to work. I promise I'll keep my eyes peeled for Omelet while I'm out patrolling." Marcus leaned down and kissed my forehead lightly.

"Can I file a report or something?" I asked weakly, already knowing the answer.

"Unfortunately you can't. Because she's a cat, there's not a lot we can do legally. I'm going to stop by a couple of shelters this afternoon, though, and I'll have a look. I'll talk to the people at the desk, and they'll keep a watch out for her, too." He squeezed my shoulder lovingly and grabbed a couple of the posters Juniper had made. "I'm also going to start hanging these up."

"Thanks, Marcus," I replied quietly. "I'm going to make some more right now." Needing to do something productive, I rose from the couch and grabbed more drawing paper and markers.

"We're going to help you, aren't we, Juniper?" Nellie said as she and Juniper joined me at the kitchen table.

After we'd made thirty more posters, Nellie, Juniper, and I plastered them throughout the city, sticking them on every available surface we could find. I handed them out to people as they passed by, asking if anyone had seen my cat, but I was only answered with sad looks and shaking heads.

The hours ticked by and I hadn't received any phone calls. As the night grew darker, I became even more worried. Omelet was out there somewhere, and she didn't even have her coat or boots. Whoever had taken her probably wasn't even giving her any tuna. Maybe they weren't feeding her at all! The possibility was almost too much for me to bear.

It was late, and I knew I needed to sleep, but the thought of curling up in my bed without Omelet purring on the pillow beside me forced a lump into my throat that wouldn't go away. Tate was on a twenty-four-hour shift, so he wasn't there to comfort me. Rather than face my lonely bed, I curled up on the couch between my aunt and my neighbor. Nellie and Juniper both sat with me, each woman trying to do her best to console me and my broken heart.

When my phone rang the next morning, I opened my eyes, surprised I was asleep on the couch. As the events of the day before crashed in my brain, my eyes once again filled with tears. I wiped them away and grabbed my phone. It was Dad.

"Good morning, Willow. Is there any news on Omelet yet?" My father's normally loud voice was softer than usual.

"How did you know about Omelet?"

"Tate called me last night and told me what happened. Have you heard any news on her whereabouts?"

"No, nothing yet." My voice quivered.

"Is there anything Elizabeth and I can do for you?"

"I don't know, Dad. I just can't believe this happened. Maybe you could hire a private detective or something?" I suggested hopefully. I knew a private detective was out of my budget.

"A private detective? For a cat? Well... I, uh... I'll look into it for you, dear."

I knew he probably thought the idea was crazy, but at that moment, I loved him for not saying so out loud. "Thanks, Dad. I'll keep you posted if we hear anything."

I hung up the phone and wondered where Nellie and Juniper had gone. They had both been beside me on the couch when I had fallen asleep. I hoped they had gotten a good night's sleep in their own beds. They took such good care of me. If it weren't for my friends and family, I knew I'd never make it through the ordeal.

My phone rang again, and I saw it was Wyatt. "Hey, Wyatt," I said as I answered.

"Morning, Willow. Have you heard anything?" His voice sounded hopeful, and I hated to crush his positive vibes.

"No, nothing yet."

"Well, I just called to tell you that I think you should stay home today. I'll take care of everything here. You have enough to worry about. And I don't want to hear any arguments from you. I'm happy to do it." Wyatt's voice told me not to argue, even though that's exactly what I wanted to do.

"As much as I want to disagree with you, you're probably right. I'm not in the right frame of mind to serve my customers today. Thank you," I replied compliantly.

"You're welcome. That's what friends are for. I've also hung about a million posters of Omelet everywhere within a three-block radius of the food truck. Someone is bound to have seen her."

"You're really the best, Wyatt. I appreciate everything you're doing for me." I brushed the tears away with the back of my hand.

"I just want her to be found safe and sound. Keep me posted," he said before hanging up.

Juniper had left a note on the kitchen counter telling me she had to go in to work early that morning. She also explained that Nellie had gone home late the previous night to get some sleep. I had strict instructions to notify both women immediately if there was any news. I headed into the bathroom for a quick shower, and began to circulate a plan of action for the day.

Since I wasn't working, I decided I would stop by the local cat lounge. I called ahead to make my reservation for noon, lucky to get a spot since it got busy around lunchtime. The trendy cat café offered food and drinks, but more importantly, it served as a hub for cat adoptions in town. I knew it was a long shot, but I thought I might find Omelet there. If someone saw her wandering around, it would be a safe place to drop her off.

I made a few more posters and hung them up on my way there, arriving at the cat lounge just before noon. After placing my order at the counter, I guzzled my drink before entering the main viewing area. Nearly a dozen cats mingled amongst the guests and played on the large structure in the center of the room. I watched as the furry felines chased cat toys, zipped across the room, and inspected their human guests. They meowed and made good use of the scratching posts. Each one was adorable.

A curious yellow kitten rubbed her body against my leg and as I leaned down to pet her, my eyes filled with tears of longing for Omelet. I wanted nothing more than to hold my baby in my arms and hear her sweet purr. Unfortunately, my hopes were quickly dashed. She wasn't among the cats at the lounge. I'd known that finding her was unlikely, but I still felt deflated.

I needed fresh air. The sounds and smells of the cat lounge were just too much. I quickly exited the café; being around other animals was a bad idea. Not knowing what else to do, and feeling more helpless by the minute, I wandered the streets of Portland, putting up more posters and looking for Omelet until the sky grew dark. When the streetlights started coming on, I knew I should head home. Tate wouldn't be back until later, but Juniper was probably wondering where I was. Feeling defeated, I dragged myself back to my apartment.

"You're here! I was so worried about you. You didn't leave me a note to tell me where you were going." Juniper gathered me into a tight hug as I entered.

"I'm sorry. I've been out looking for Omelet all day. I don't know what else to do, June. I even went to the cat lounge, hoping I might find her there. I didn't." I dropped my weary body onto the couch and Juniper sat beside me.

"We're going to find her." She bobbed her head up and down. "You know, I was thinking. A friend of mine who lives in the homeless camp is an animal psychic. Maybe she can pick up on Omelet's aura and tell us where she is."

"Her aura?" I raised my eyebrow skeptically. I wasn't one to dismiss other people's beliefs, but that seemed a bit out there, even for me.

"Yes, Willow. Open your mind. Expand your horizons. My friend is very gifted." Juniper patted my hand before continuing. "Also, I've seen cats all over the homeless camps in town. The people there are very kind. If she's wandered into one of them, someone will take care of her."

Juniper probably believed she was making me feel better by assuring me that someone would take care of Omelet if she was out there, but the thought of my baby wandering around the scary streets of Portland made my stomach churn with nervousness. Omelet wasn't used to fending for herself, and she didn't like strangers. She was probably terrified.

Juniper's right. Omelet might be in one of the homeless camps. If she is, I have to find out. I need to go there. I knew Tate would kill me if I even thought about looking for my cat in the homeless camps, but at that point, I was willing to try anything. *What Tate doesn't know won't hurt him.*

But no sooner had the thought entered my head that I knew it was a bad idea. If I was going to go out looking, I needed to take Tate or Juniper with me. Sometimes I had to remind myself that I wasn't alone anymore. I had people who cared about me, and I didn't need to go rogue.

"Thanks, Juniper. I'm just so worried, and I don't know what to do, you know?" I rotated my shoulders in an attempt to loosen the tension that had taken up residence there.

"I'll tell you what we're going to do. I'm going to fix you a nice drink, and we're going to do some yoga. I can see from the way you're holding your shoulders that your body is one giant ball of stress. We're going to work that out." Juniper patted my leg, rose from the couch, and went into the kitchen.

She opened the cupboard, and I spotted various jars and containers filled with oils, herbs, and natural healing remedies. Having grown up in a commune, Juniper had a fondness for herbal potions. Most of them had been purchased in the last few days from the apothecary next to her yoga studio. I had absolutely no idea what was in those bottles, and I was a little afraid to find out.

"June, what kind of drink are you fixing me?" I wasn't completely paranoid, but I did like to know what I was consuming. "It's nothing illegal, is it?"

"This is Portland, Willow. Very few things are illegal. Don't worry." Juniper mixed several substances together, then came back into the living room and handed me some sort of potion. "Drink it. It's an herbal elixir. You'll be relaxed in no time."

I sniffed the drink and shrugged. *How bad can it be?* I downed it in a few gulps. "Now what?"

Juniper scooted my coffee table to the side and created a large, open space on my living room floor where she placed two foamy yoga mats. She lit several lavender-scented candles, turned on soothing meditation music, and turned off all the lights in the apartment. "Now we're going to do yoga."

"I don't mean to be a skeptic, Juniper, but I don't think herbal potions and yoga are going to help me relax and go to sleep. My cat is missing, and I'm way too stressed out."

"Don't be such a pessimist. Just humor me," Juniper encouraged.

"All right, I'll go along with whatever you say. I suppose that drink wasn't too bad."

"I'm going to lead you through a Shakti mudra. It's a pose that will help induce rest. Once I'm through with you, you'll sleep like a baby." Juniper motioned for me to follow her lead. "This would be better if we had a few goats, but we'll just have to make do."

"Goats would be nice." I stood beside her and watched her closely.

"Yes, goat yoga is quite therapeutic," she replied with a nod.

"I imagine it is. What now?"

"Sit on the floor. Close your eyes. Turn your palms to face each other." Juniper spoke softly, and I did as she instructed. "Now join the tips of your ring fingers and your pinkies. Fold your thumbs into your palms and cover with your index and middle fingers. We're going to relax, breathe deeply, and hold our hands in front of our hearts for five minutes."

"Five minutes seems like a long time, June," I argued as I opened one eye and peeked at her.

"Close your eyes and trust me. If you do it right, the time will fly right by."

I closed my eyes and did as Juniper instructed, listening to the soothing, meditative music floating through the air. I tried to clear my mind of all stress, and much to my surprise, it actually worked.

After what seemed like only a few seconds, Juniper told me that five minutes had passed. My eyelids were heavy, my body felt warm, and my brain was drowsy. I wanted nothing more than to crawl into my bed and sleep for a week.

"I'm really tired now," I said groggily.

"I know. I'm going to help you up, and you're going to get into bed." Juniper gently helped me to my feet, led me to my room, and tucked me into bed.

"Did you drug me?" I tried to keep my eyes open, but I was finding it nearly impossible to do so.

"You've released all the tension from your body, that's all." She patted my cheek and kissed me on the forehead. "Sleep now, Willow."

CHAPTER FIFTEEN

"Morning, babe." Tate scooted next to me in the bed, and my eyes fluttered open as I felt his hot breath on my neck.

"Hey, is it morning already? I didn't hear you come in last night." I turned my body toward his and snuggled into his arms. It felt so good to have him close to me.

"I'm not surprised that you didn't hear me come in. When I got home, you were basically comatose. I actually checked your pulse when I climbed into bed." He grinned and playfully nibbled my earlobe, causing goose bumps to erupt on every inch of my flesh.

I might have been comatose when Tate came home, but I was pretty sure my pulse was working just fine at that moment. In fact, as he kissed me, I felt it inch up a notch or two.

"Hmm, I think Juniper drugged me with something she called an herbal elixir. I'm sort of curious what the herbs were. Then she turned my body into rubber with some kind of weird hippie yoga. I'm pretty sure she's a witch doctor. But the good news is I'm not comatose now. What do you say we pick up where we left off the other day?" I kissed him tenderly and tried to clear my brain of everything else for a few minutes.

"Are you sure? I know you're a bit scattered with everything going on, and that's okay. You don't have to put on a brave front for me," he replied as he held me closely and stroked my back.

"I'm always amazed at how well you get me. No matter what else is going on, I want you to know that I'd be lost without you. I know I haven't been a very good fiancée lately." I brushed my fingers lightly across his cheek and kissed him again, more deeply than before. "But I love you so much."

As concerned as I was about Omelet being missing, I knew Tate deserved my undivided attention for at least a little while. We'd been having some trouble connecting, and I knew the fault was mine. Relationships only worked when both people contributed, and I hadn't been pulling my weight lately. Tate was always the giver, and I did nothing but take.

If I wanted to hold on to him, that needed to change. Even though I was conflicted about marriage, there wasn't a single doubt that I loved him. Tate was far too kind to say that I'd been neglectful, but I didn't need him to tell me what I already knew. I pushed my worry for Omelet aside for a moment and vowed to give Tate my complete focus. I was worried about finding my girl, but I was just as worried about losing the man I loved.

I touched my lips to his and reveled in the way that it felt to kiss him. For just a few minutes, I tried to only focus on the good thing that was right in front of me. Everything else in my life might have been wrong, but being with Tate was right.

"Hey, Wyatt," I said as I made my way into the Dancing Crêpe later that morning.

Tate and I had finally managed to spend some quality time together, and although I was still worried about Omelet, my soul was a bit more settled. I didn't know how, but I was more determined than ever to find my baby. I just had to keep telling myself that everything was going to be fine.

"Willow, you're back." Wyatt gathered me into a tight hug. "I thought you might take the day off again."

"No, I need to be here. I can't bear another second of sitting around twiddling my thumbs at home and thinking about Omelet. I have to keep busy. It's the only way I won't lose my mind." I dropped my bag on the floor and tied my mint-green apron around my waist.

"How are you holding up? Sorry, I hate that question, but I don't know what else to say. I'm worried about you." Wyatt mixed crêpe batter as he talked.

"I miss Omelet like mad. I don't really know what to do without her." I grabbed my inventory sheet and took stock of the ingredients on the shelf, trying to avoid looking too long at Omelet's crate in the corner. Seeing her things was just too hard.

As I went over the list, a wave of nausea nearly made my knees buckle. I took a deep breath and tried to still my churning stomach. I'd been feeling awful for the past few days. I was sure it was because of the stress of losing Omelet. Or perhaps it had something to do with the mysterious herbal elixir I'd consumed the night before.

"We're going to find her, Willow," Wyatt continued. "Don't lose faith yet."

"I'm trying really hard not to," I answered as I placed my hand on my stomach and begged it to stop spinning.

Wyatt chopped strawberries and placed them into the refrigerator, then grabbed bananas and began slicing them. The sweet scent wafted into my nostrils, and I pushed down the urge to vomit. Beads of perspiration condensed on my upper lip, and I wondered when it had gotten so hot.

What is wrong with me?

I took a deep breath and tried to ignore the fact that I felt horrible. "I haven't given up, but I'm really worried. The longer she's gone, the less likely we are to find her." I scribbled a grocery list onto a piece of paper. "And I have to find her."

Wyatt nodded and smiled comfortingly at me. I finished the list and put it into my purse, making a mental note that I needed to stop by the grocery store on my way home. As I did, I noticed a medium-sized manila envelope with my name written in large, bold letters across the front. It was lying on the shelf next to the cupboard. Picking it up, I examined it closely. It felt like there was something bulky inside.

"Where did this envelope come from, Wyatt?" I asked as I opened the seal.

"It was on the stairs when I arrived this morning. I didn't see who left it." His back was turned toward me as he continued slicing different kinds of fruit and placing them into various containers.

What could this possibly be? My pulse beat rapidly as I held the envelope. Something told me that whatever was inside was bad, and although I was curious, I was also afraid to look.

Finally working up the nerve to glance at the contents, I did my best to stifle the gasp that escaped. I pulled out the sheet of paper that was folded neatly on top of Omelet's rhinestone collar. As I began to read, my heart sank.

I HAVE YOUR CAT. IF YOU WANT TO SEE HER ALIVE AGAIN, meet me in front of the gas station on Broadway at eleven o'clock this morning. Come alone, and bring $1000.00. If you don't follow these instructions exactly, you'll be sorry.

MY HANDS SHOOK AS I QUICKLY SHOVED THE PAPER back inside of the envelope. I tenderly ran my fingers across Omelet's collar and reminded myself that I could not cry at that moment. If I was going to rescue my cat, I couldn't let Wyatt or anyone else know that anything was wrong. The note said to come alone, so that's what I had to do. I also needed to get my hands on a thousand dollars. That amount was going to set me back quite a bit, but Omelet was worth every penny.

No one can know about any of this.

I opened my handbag and placed the envelope inside. Checking the clock on the wall, I saw it was already ten fifteen. I needed to get going if I had any hope of getting across town in time, especially considering I had to stop at the bank first. Luckily, my bank was on the way.

"Hey, Wyatt, I forgot something at home. Do you think you'll be all right here for a bit if I go?" I tried to control the trembling in my voice.

"Sure, Willow, do whatever you need to do. I've got it under control." He briefly glanced my way and gave me a strange look, as if he knew something was up.

"Thanks. I'll be back soon." The faster I made a break

for it, the less likely he was to figure out that anything was wrong.

Grabbing my bag, I quickly dashed out of the food truck, once again pushing down the waves of nausea that threatened to make me lose my breakfast. Doing my best to control my frenzied thoughts and the beating of my heart, I ran to the bus stop, jumped on the MAX, and rode it across town.

I hopped off at the stop next to my bank and ran inside. Filling out the withdrawal slip with trembling hands wasn't easy, and my handwriting looked sloppy and hasty. I grabbed my driver's license, slid it and the paper across the counter toward the overly perky teller, and smiled weakly. She punched some keys on the computer, went to the back to grab my money, and then proceeded to count the stack of hundred-dollar bills for me.

That's a lot of cash. My bank account is going to look pretty bleak after this.

Reminding myself that the money wasn't as important as getting Omelet back, I ran to the bus stop and jumped back on. The MAX seemed to be moving much slower than usual, and I urged it to hurry. When we reached the stop near the gas station that was indicated in the ransom note, I jumped from my seat and ran down the aisle. My only thought was getting to Omelet in time, and I nearly knocked a man over in my haste.

My feet hit the sidewalk and I began running toward the gas station. It was only a block away, and I could almost see it. My shoes pounded on the pavement as my legs propelled me forward. I saw the store's neon sign and made myself run faster. As I approached, I heard a loud meow, and I gasped when I saw Omelet tied to a tree in the back alley behind the building.

"Omelet, I'm coming," I yelled loudly.

She saw me and howled in response. My lungs were on fire as I collapsed on the pavement next to her. I began untying the rope that held her in place, doing my best to see through the deluge of tears that clouded my eyes and ran down my cheeks.

How could anyone do this to my baby?

Omelet meowed even louder as I fumbled with the knotted rope. "I've almost got you, baby. You're going to be okay now."

Finally, the rope came loose and Omelet was free. I scooped her up and hugged her tightly, thankful to have found her.

Suddenly, I felt a thud on the back of my head, and as the sound reverberated in my brain, everything around me faded to black.

CHAPTER SIXTEEN

My eyes fluttered open and I took a quick look around. *This is not my room. I'm not in my apartment. Am I dreaming?* I had no idea where I was, but my head was pounding, and the ever-present nausea was about a million times worse. The strange room was spinning. I took a few slow, deep breaths in an attempt to calm down and figure out what I was going to do next.

Omelet was curled in a ball on the pillow next to me sleeping soundly. She didn't appear to be hurt, and she seemed to be resting comfortably. *Wasn't she just tied to a tree? What is happening? This is really weird.* I had no idea what had transpired back at the gas station, but I remembered the thud I'd taken to the head, and the way my poor cat had been treated. Unless this was some sort of freaky nightmare, I knew something was very wrong. I had obviously been knocked out and moved against my will.

I looked at my surroundings, and much to my surprise, I discovered I wasn't being held captive in a dungeon or a cell. The room wasn't cold and dank but was instead warm, cozy, and nicely decorated. There were paintings with scenes of beautiful landscapes on the light blue walls, and a vase of fresh wildflowers brightened the antique bedside table next to me. An overstuffed leather chair sat in the corner next to a bookshelf filled with literary classics, and a royal blue, fuzzy blanket was folded neatly on its arm. There was even a steaming mug of hot tea next to the wildflowers, although I certainly wasn't crazy enough to take a drink of it.

Omelet remained asleep, perfectly at home in our strange surroundings. I wondered if this was where she'd been taken when she was catnapped. If so, it didn't seem too bad, although I still had no idea why it had happened in the first place.

Moving slowly, I scooted out of bed and tiptoed to the window. Pulling aside the cheery cotton curtains, I glanced through the windowpanes to see if I could find any clues as to our whereabouts. Nothing looked familiar. There were no tall buildings, no busy Portland streets, and no hubbub of urban activity.

It looked like we were in the suburbs. I wasn't in the city anymore. When I glanced around the room for my bag, my heart sank when I couldn't find it anywhere. I dropped to my knees and looked under the bed, opened all the dresser drawers, and scoured the contents of the closet, but it was nowhere to be found. That meant I didn't have my phone, and without my phone, I was going to have a hard time calling for help.

"Oh good, you're up. I was worried when I couldn't wake you. I thought perhaps I had bonked you on the head a little bit harder than I intended." The voice, somehow vaguely familiar, floated into the room before the woman herself did.

Turning around, I gasped in shock when I saw my

captor. "Diana! What...? Where...? I don't understand," I stammered as I stared into the face of Diana Wilmington Simpson, or, as I had always called her, Step-Monster Number Two.

Diana had been married to Dad when I was a teenager. She wasn't much older than me, and she was just barely past her own teenage years when she walked down the aisle with my father. She was a petulant, selfish, awful woman, and I had celebrated the day she and my father divorced. We hadn't gotten along well when she was my stepmother, and I didn't hold out much hope that our relationship was about to change, seeing as how she'd knocked me out and kidnapped me.

She smiled slyly, and a thousand bad memories came rushing back to me, particularly the time that I had caught her coming on to Tate. I had walked into the boathouse and found her, wearing next to nothing, with her body all over a very cornered teenage Tate. He had tried to be nice to her, and she had gotten the wrong idea. Thinking about that devil woman's hands on my fiancé made my blood boil, even though it happened many years ago when Tate and I weren't together.

Diana gave me a once-over, and I stared right back at her, refusing to be intimidated. "It's been a while, hasn't it, Willow?"

"Yeah, it's been ten years since I've seen you, thank goodness." I collapsed into the leather chair as shock, anger, and confusion made my legs feel like rubber.

Diana seated her voluptuous, nearly six-foot frame on the edge of the bed in front of me and turned her cool blue eyes in my direction. She crossed her mile-long legs and smoothed her jet-black hair. A former plus-sized model, Diana was beautiful, and the passage of ten years hadn't diminished her looks in the slightest. She hated me when she and my father were married, and she'd done all she could to make my life miserable.

Good old Dad had always known how to pick the vipers.

"I suppose you're wondering why you're here," she continued.

"You could say that. Are you the one who smacked me in the head? I'm sure that's something you've always wanted to do." I eyed her angrily.

"Ah, I see you haven't changed all that much since you were a bratty teenager. You still have the same sharp tongue." Diana smirked at me and batted her spidery eyelashes.

"Why are you doing this? Why did you take Omelet? What on earth could you possibly want with my cat?"

Upon hearing my words, Omelet opened her eyes, yawned, stretched, and looked back and forth between me and Diana. I rose from the chair and faced my captor.

"Come on, Willow, are you really that dense? I have little to no interest in your cat. She was merely a ploy to get to you." Diana stood as well and moved closer to me. "And it was so easy. I was able to lure her out of her little basket with the promise of a few cat treats. You were so distracted that you didn't even notice."

I'd forgotten just how tall she was. I squared my shoulders and tried to make myself look larger, but it was no use. She was an Amazon woman, and she towered over me. *No wonder she had no trouble knocking me out and moving my scrawny little body.*

"Okay, Diana, you've made your point. You're in charge here. What do you want with me? If you wanted to invite me over for tea, all you had to do was ask. Of course, since

I've always hated you, I probably would have said no." I smirked and refused to back down.

"Oh, Willow, you're so cute. You see, you're going to help me get what I want. You're quite a useful part of my plan, and I intend to utilize you to the fullest extent." Diana placed her hands on her hips, and I noticed the butt of a small handgun sticking out of her pocket.

"What is it you think I can do for you?" I tried not to let my voice belie the fact that I was very afraid.

Although I knew my captor, I was fully aware that I was in a dangerous predicament. No one knew where I was, and from the cold look in Diana's crystal-blue eyes, I had the feeling that she might be a little crazy, not to mention the fact that she had a gun.

"You're going to make me rich, Willow Simpson. That's what you're going to do for me." Her eyes glazed over a little more and she sneered at me.

"That's actually pretty funny. You've obviously failed to do the proper research. In case you didn't know, I don't have a ton of money. I own a food truck, and while it's been pretty successful, it definitely hasn't made me rich. In fact, the thousand dollars I withdrew for you today pretty much drained me. I'm going to assume you found the money in my bag, wherever that is." She obviously hadn't thoroughly investigated this little scheme of hers.

"You may not have money, but it's no secret that your father is one of the richest men in the world. I should know —I was married to him." Diana rolled her eyes and once again seated herself on the edge of the bed.

Not knowing what to do, I returned to the leather chair in the corner. *Just keep her talking, Willow. As long as that gun doesn't come out, you're golden.*

"What does Dad's money have to do with me? It's not

like I have access to it or anything." Her plan still wasn't making any sense to me.

"You are your father's only child, and from what I remember, he cares very deeply for you. Of course, he wasn't one to show it much, but I knew the truth. He would have done anything for you, and I'm sure that's still the case. At least, that's what I'm banking on." She examined her nails, and I noticed that she was in need of a manicure. "So, I'm sure that when I let him know he'd better pay up or I'll get rid of you, he'll be fairly prompt with his reply."

"You mean you're going to kill me if Dad doesn't give you money?" My heart began to race when I realized she was being deadly serious. "How much are you trying to get from him?"

"Oh, only five million. That's pocket change for a man like your father. And besides, I'm sure his only daughter is well worth the price. At least you'd better hope that's what he says." She held my gaze with her penetrating stare.

"Why do you want his money, Diana? Didn't you get enough in the divorce settlement? Have you gone through all of it already?" I needed to get more information.

"Divorce settlement? You're not very smart, are you, Willow? Your father made me sign a prenuptial agreement, and I got nothing. If it wasn't for the fact that I had a lucrative modeling career before I met him, I would have been sent away penniless. Luckily I had my own savings account, although that's pretty much dried up at this point." She shook her head in disbelief, as if her plight in this world couldn't get any worse.

"It doesn't look like you're exactly homeless, Diana. I assume this is your house, right? And although it may not be the mansion you lived in with Dad, it's not a slum."

"It's a rental house in Vancouver, Willow. Vancouver!"

Diana yelled. "A woman like me does not deserve to live in Vancouver."

"Is that where we are?" I tried to sound casual, but I was sure she could hear the surprise in my voice.

Hearing that we were in Vancouver was great news. At least I was still fairly close to home. I didn't know what I was supposed to do with the knowledge, but at least I had found out where I was.

Vancouver, Washington was just across the bridge from Portland, Oregon, and although I had been there a few times, I didn't know much about the city. If I could make a break from the house, I would eventually be able to find my way back home, but it wasn't going to be easy, especially without my phone.

"Yes, Willow, we are in Vancouver, or Vantucky, as I like to call it."

"You know, I just read an article that said Vancouver was the most hipster city in America. It can't be all that bad, Diana," I offered with a shrug.

"Vancouver is an awful place, Willow, and it's where I've been for the last ten years. I've had to endure it ever since your father discarded me and left me a pauper, all because he found out about a silly little fling I had with a photographer," Diana answered with a flip of her shiny hair.

"A silly little fling? Is that what you're calling it now? You were engaged to another man behind Dad's back! What did you expect would happen when he found out?" I rolled my eyes at the obviously insane woman sitting in front of me. "I'm sorry, Diana, but you're not a pauper. Things could be so much worse for you than they are." I thought of my aunt Juniper living on the streets all those years.

"Perhaps, but things could also be a lot better for me.

And they will be once I get that five million from your father. I'll finally get to live the kind of life a woman like me deserves." She smoothed her hair and examined her chipped nail polish. From the looks of her hands, I was guessing a manicure was one of the first things on her to-do list once she was a millionaire.

"Well, what now, Diana? Have you called Dad and told him your demands yet?"

I tried to guess how Dad would react when he heard what Diana wanted from him. He'd been so angry when he'd divorced her, and I could only imagine how furious he was going to be when he found out what she'd done to me. Although I was trying not to appear flustered, I secretly hoped that Diana had already received a response back from him. I didn't really have a plan, and I prayed she was going to tell me that Dad was on his way with the money.

"No, I haven't contacted him just yet. You see, I had to make sure you woke up first. You scared me a little bit when you wouldn't come to. I had to hit you pretty hard to knock you out, and then you just stayed asleep. I needed to make sure you didn't die before I sent the ransom note." She shrugged nonchalantly, as if she were discussing the weather instead of the fact that she had knocked me out, kidnapped, and nearly killed me.

"Okay...." It wasn't very often that I was at a loss for words, but I honestly had no idea how I was supposed to respond to the mentally disturbed woman.

"So here's what we're going to do. I'll write the note now, and then I have a friend who'll pick it up and deliver it for me. I expect we'll hear from good old Barringer pretty quickly after he receives it, and you and I will just hang out here and wait for his answer. I'm sure we have a lot of things we can catch up on. But for your sake, you'd better hope he does what I say and decides to meet me at the designated spot. *Alone.* If he's stupid enough to call the police, this isn't going to end well for you. He has forty-eight hours. If I don't get a reply, I'll have no choice but to kill you."

Diana rose from the bed, patted the gun in her pocket, gave me a quick little wave, and exited the bedroom.

My stomach churned and my head spun wildly. *How in the world am I going to get myself out of this mess?* Five million dollars was a lot of money, even for a man like Dad. He and I hadn't always seen eye to eye, and he was probably still mad at me for riding my bike naked through the city of Portland. What if he decided that he didn't want to part with that much money on my behalf? What if he'd finally had enough of my antics and decided I wasn't worth five million dollars?

"Oh, Omelet, we'd better hope he comes through for us. If not, we are officially out of luck."

I sat on the couch opposite my captor, literally twiddling my thumbs. It was dark in the room, with only the flickering light of the television to illuminate my surroundings. Almost forty-six hours had passed since Diana's friend delivered the ransom note, and she said she still hadn't received an answer from Dad. I was doing my best to portray a calm demeanor on the outside, but on the inside, I was terrified.

My worst fears were coming true. My father wasn't going to rescue me this time around. I had obviously spent all my chances with him. I'd always known that I wasn't super high on his list of importance, but I figured that Dad would at least come through for me if it meant keeping me alive. The realization that he didn't care whether I lived or died stung more deeply that I would ever let on.

Diana hadn't hurt me, other than the whack to my head when she'd taken me, but I had no doubt that she would be true to her word the second we reached the forty-eight-hour mark. The handgun on the coffee table in front of her was a stark reminder of the dangerous situation. If Dad wasn't going to rescue me, then I had no other choice. I was going to have to figure out a way to get Omelet and myself out of the mess.

Running through a list of possible escape plans, I managed to find something wrong with each and every plot. I realized I didn't have a lot of options, but I refused to give up. I reminded myself that this wasn't the first time I'd had to deal with a deranged lunatic who wanted me dead. I had no idea how I kept ending up in such predicaments, but I was going to do my best to get out of alive.

"Willow, bring me two ibuprofen from the bathroom medicine cabinet. My head is killing me," Diana barked.

"You could ask nicely," I retorted sarcastically.

Diana's eyes flashed with anger, and she grabbed the gun and pointed it at me. "Go get me two ibuprofen. Now!"

I wasn't usually too keen on the idea of following orders, especially those given by my former stepmothers, but seeing as how she clearly held all the cards in our present situation, and given the fact that she had no qualms about killing me, I did as she asked.

I went into the bathroom, opened the medicine cabinet, and found the ibuprofen. Unscrewing the lid, I poured two capsules into my hand and was just about to shut the door when I saw it. I could almost hear the angelic choir singing the "Hallelujah" chorus. *Bingo!* Grabbing the orange prescription bottle, I read the label as a distant memory floated to the surface.

I remembered Mrs. Bates, our family's housekeeper, showing me the bottle when I was younger and explaining that I should never take the pills inside of it. She'd told me that Diana had a lot of anxiety, which led to trouble sleeping. Because of her insomnia, her doctor had prescribed a pretty heavy-duty sleeping pill.

Mrs. Bates said the medication was incredibly potent. In her words, the pills were strong enough to tranquilize a horse. Upon penalty of death, she warned me that I should leave the medicine alone. I had seen the pills in action a few times, and I remembered that when Diana took them, they basically knocked her out cold.

As the idea began to form in my head, I grinned. *That woman is going to get exactly what she deserves, and I'm going to be the one to give it to her.* I opened the lid and dumped two pills into my hand. I dropped them into my pocket and replaced the bottle in the medicine cabinet. Smiling to myself, I headed back into the living room where Diana was still engrossed in the gory movie.

"Here you go, Diana," I said as I dropped the ibuprofen into her hands. I noticed the handgun was strategically placed across her lap for easy access. "You know, you should take those with some food. Why don't I make us something to eat? I'm a pretty good cook, you know."

"You want to cook for me?" Diana popped the ibuprofen into her mouth and washed them down with a swig from the bottle of wine on the coffee table.

"Cooking is what I do best. I'll just have a look around the kitchen and whip something up. By the way, have you heard from Dad?" I already knew the answer, but I wanted her to believe that I was still holding out hope for dear old Dad.

"No, unfortunately for you, I haven't. It's quite sad, don't you think? Your own father won't give up a little of his money to keep you alive." Her voice wafted into the kitchen where I was prepping the food.

"Honestly, Diana, I'm not surprised. You seem to think that Dad cares about my well-being much more than he actually does." I chopped some vegetables, cooked pasta, and poured another glass of wine for Diana. I was going to make this a meal she would never forget.

Once the pasta primavera was prepared, I grabbed two colorful plates from the cabinet. Diana's plate was bright green, and mine was orange. *Just be sure you don't mix up the plates, Willow, or your goose is cooked!* I reached into my pocket and retrieved the two sleeping pills. Crushing the medicine, I sprinkled it onto Diana's food, stirring it well so it wouldn't be seen. I mixed it into the flavorful sauce, hopeful that she wouldn't discover it until it was too late. I crossed my fingers and prayed my plan would work.

"Dinner's ready, Diana. Would you like me to bring it to you so you can eat while you finish your movie?" I called from the kitchen.

"Sure," she replied.

"Coming right up!" I arranged the food and a fresh glass of wine on a tray I found in the cupboard and carried it in to her. She leaned forward and placed the gun on the coffee table next to her bottle of wine. "Here you go. I hope you enjoy it." I smiled widely.

"Why are you being so nice to me? What are you up to?" Diana's skeptical eyes met mine.

"I'm not up to anything. I've just been giving your situation some thought, and I really hope your plan works out. I mean, you were married to Dad, after all. You should have gotten some of his money. I want to see that you get exactly what you deserve." I grinned innocently and returned to the kitchen to eat my own food while I waited for the pills to kick in.

"This is delicious, Willow. It's no wonder your food truck is so popular," Diana said between bites of pasta.

"Thank you. Cooking is my passion. I'm pretty good at

it," I agreed. *Sometimes I even add special surprise ingredients.*

"So tell me, what ever happened to your friend Tate? I've always wondered what became of that handsome boy." Diana continued to shove large bites of food into her mouth. "He was a looker when he was a teenager. I'll bet money he's simply delicious as a grown man."

I felt my anger rise, but I tried to keep a handle on it. "Tate is actually my fiancé."

"Oh my, you're a lucky woman. I'll bet he's quite the catch. If your dad doesn't come through for you and I end up having to kill you, I'll be sure to look him up. I'm guessing he'll need a bit of consoling once you're gone." She glanced toward me, but I avoided her gaze.

How dare she talk about Tate that way. If she so much as looks in his direction, I'm going to lose it.

I scooped up large bites of pasta and devoured every last morsel. Diana had gone back to watching her movie, and I kept my eye on her as I dished another pile of food onto my plate.

I'm hungry all the time lately. It must be my nerves. I think I've turned into a stress eater.

I watched closely as Diana finished her plate of food and sipped her glass of wine, wondering how long it took for those sleeping pills to do the trick. The recommended dosage was just one pill, but I'd given her two for good measure. I wanted to be sure she was down for the count so Omelet and I would have plenty of time to escape.

I didn't have to wonder for very long, because not even five minutes later, Diana's wineglass slipped from her hand and crashed to the floor as her body slumped over on the couch. I waited for two full minutes before I tiptoed into the living room, bent down, shook her gently, and called her name.

When the only response was a string of drool coming from her slack mouth, I knew the time had come to make my escape. Diana didn't have a home phone, and she'd done a good job of hiding both her cell phone and computer from me. I hadn't managed to find my bag, so I had no form of communication. Omelet and I were on our own.

"Come on, Omelet, we're leaving. Whatever's out there is far less dangerous than what's in here."

I grabbed my cat and ran out the front door.

CHAPTER EIGHTEEN

The night was fairly warm, so at least I didn't have to worry about the possibility of freezing to death. Holding Omelet in my arms, I ran for several blocks before I stopped to take a breath. When I spotted a bench, I collapsed onto it and worked to calm the racing of my heart. Glancing around, I tried to find anything that looked familiar, but I was out of luck. I'd only been in Vancouver a handful of times, so everything was foreign.

I might as well be in Timbuktu.

Having no clue where Diana's house was located, I was completely disoriented. I didn't know if I was one mile or twenty from the Interstate Bridge. All I knew was I had to find it. To top it all off, I think I had eaten the pasta primavera too quickly, because it was threatening to come back up. I wasn't sure what that was all about. Maybe I needed to see a doctor when I finally made it back home.

Knowing I shouldn't waste another second, I stood and continued walking. It was dark, I was tired, and other than Omelet, I was all alone. Trying to push down the desperation I was beginning to feel, I turned my thoughts to Tate. I knew without a doubt that he was beside himself with worry for me by that point, and I wanted nothing more than to be in his arms.

I needed to find a way to call him. I supposed I could have stopped someone on the street and asked to use a phone, but I came to the conclusion that it wasn't the best plan of action. Having too much contact with strangers at night in an unknown place was basically just asking for trouble. I needed to find out where I was and get back to Portland.

Walking past a convenience store, I decided I would go inside and ask for help. The neighborhood seemed sketchy, but I couldn't be too choosy.

"Excuse me, sir, but do you have a phone I can use?" I asked the man behind the counter.

"Why do you need a phone?" He frowned.

"I need to call my fiancé."

"Don't you have a cell phone? I thought everyone had a cell phone these days."

"If I had a phone, do you think I would be asking to use yours? Never mind, can you just call the police for me? I need help."

"The police? Listen, lady, I don't want any trouble here." He raised a skeptical eyebrow at me.

"I'm not trying to cause trouble. I'm *in* trouble!"

As the words came out, a man walked through the front door of the store. I covered my mouth to stifle the gasp that escaped. It was Diana's friend, the man who came to her house to pick up the ransom letter! I knew if he saw me it was all over. He hadn't yet recognized me, so I turned around and sprinted out the front door, running until I couldn't run anymore. Looking behind me, I hadn't been followed, so I came to a halt and tried to catch my breath and formulate a plan.

If I had money and a phone, I would just call a cab, but without my bag, I had no way to pay the fare. *Ironic, isn't it? The daughter of one of the richest men in the world can't afford cab fare.*

Thinking of Dad made my heart ache. I couldn't believe that he hadn't come through for me. I'd been trying to wrap my brain around the fact that he would rather have me dead than part with his precious money. The knowledge of how little I meant to him cut me to the core.

Pushing those thoughts aside, I pictured my cozy apartment. All I wanted was to rewind things and be back at home before this whole mess happened. I had led a pretty charmed life up to that point, but somehow I had gotten a bit off track the past few months. Rather than taking the time to appreciate all the things I had, like my fantastic fiancé, I had done nothing but question our relationship and find problems where there were none.

I missed Tate dreadfully, and more than anything I wanted to see his face again. This whole crazy situation had shown me one thing—the only future I cared about was one with Tate. My worry about our relationship changing seemed trivial to me in the grand scheme of things. After all I had been through the past few days, I just wanted to grab hold of the happiness that Tate was offering me.

Sure, I was still afraid. With my history, I probably always would be. But I knew that even as scared as I was, I was ready to become his wife. If Tate still wanted to get married in October, I would drop to my knees and thank my lucky stars. I vowed to get to work planning the wedding right away. I wasn't letting my happy ending slip through my fingers. Nothing else mattered to me.

Omelet squirmed in my arms and I adjusted my hold on her. We had been walking for quite a while, and my feet were killing me, but I continued on. I didn't have her leash, so carrying her was the only option. I wasn't going to risk losing her after I'd finally found her.

Glancing up, I smiled with relief when I saw the Interstate Bridge ahead of me. A renewed sense of purpose washed over me when I realized that it wouldn't be long until I made it back home. Walking from Vancouver to Portland wasn't ideal, but I knew I could do it.

I crossed the bridge carefully, the roaring water of the Columbia River raging below me. I kept repeating over and over that I could make it home. I had no idea exactly how far I had come, but I was certain it had been several miles.

The image of Tate's worried face in my mind allowed me to keep putting one foot in front of the other. Before long, the lights of the city grew brighter, and I knew I was getting closer. Looking at the street signs, I realized I was back inside Portland's city limits.

Walking down the familiar streets, waves of relief washed over me. I kept traveling, even though the queasiness in my stomach made me feel like I was about to lose my dinner. I watched as several cabs flew by me, and I wished more than anything that I had some money so I could get one of them to take me home.

My pace was slowing, but still, I continued. When I saw I was only a few blocks away from the Dancing Crêpe, I got excited. Unfortunately, I didn't have my keys, and without them, I couldn't even get inside my own food truck without breaking and entering. I didn't have my bus pass, so public transportation was out as well.

I didn't know what time it was, but it had to be well past midnight at that point. Because of the late hour, none of the businesses were open. I began to see more and more homeless people camped out on the sidewalk, tucked into sleeping bags or propped against buildings for the night. They looked cold, tired, hungry, and desperate. I reminded myself that my plight was only temporary; most of the people on the streets didn't have that consolation. I'd never given much thought to the homeless community before I met Juniper, but I noticed them more and more these days.

As a wave of nausea nearly took my breath away, I reached out to steady myself, resting my hand on the building beside me. My head began to spin, and the dinner I'd been trying so hard to keep down finally came back up. I took deep breaths and did my best to stay upright, but before I knew what was happening, my body collapsed.

Sitting on the sidewalk, I drew my knees up toward my chest and cradled Omelet in the space between. I was exhausted from walking so far, not to mention the fact that I felt gross because I had just vomited. I was sicker than I could ever remember.

I needed help, and I needed it immediately, but I had no way of reaching anyone I knew. Tears streamed down my cheeks and I pulled Omelet even closer. "I don't know what to do, baby. I just want to go home. I just want Tate."

"What are you doing down there?" I looked up and saw a man standing above me.

Fear overtook me. I stared into the face of the stranger, attempting to smile but knowing the effort was mostly in vain. I prayed that he didn't want to hurt me, because I knew there was no way I could fight back.

The stranger was very thin, and I wondered how long it had been since he'd had a decent meal. He had long, scraggly hair that looked like it hadn't been washed for weeks, and his tattered clothing looked even worse than his hair.

"I'm not feeling well," I began.

I swallowed hard over the lump in my throat. At that point, I was so weak that I could barely get the words out.

"You shouldn't be out here alone at night. It's not safe." He reached into his pocket for something and as he did, panic overtook me.

The man was right; it wasn't safe out there on the streets alone in the middle of the night. I had the sinking feeling that I'd just escaped one awful situation only to wander into an even worse one. The man was more than likely reaching into his pocket for a knife or a gun. I was clearly going to die right there on the sidewalk, and I couldn't even fight back.

I closed my eyes and braced myself for what was about to happen. As my mind raced with all the horrible alternatives, the exhaustion, dizziness, nausea, and panic got the best of me and I passed out.

CHAPTER NINETEEN

"Well good morning, miss. I was wondering when you might decide to rejoin the land of the living."

Waking up to the sound of a strange man's voice wasn't something to which I was accustomed, but after the events of the night before, I congratulated myself on the fact that I'd managed to wake up at all.

Opening my eyes, I tried to figure out what was going on.

I had a vague recollection of having seen the disheveled-looking man the night before. He was the stranger who'd reached into his pocket for an unknown object right before my brain and stomach got the better of me, and I passed out. Since I was still alive, I assumed that he hadn't meant me any harm.

I sat up slowly and felt a rush of relief when I saw Omelet in the corner nibbling on some cat food. I didn't know where I was, so I tried to gain my composure. Smoothing my wayward hair, I rubbed the sleep from my eyes and allowed my body a moment to stretch. As I did so, I looked closely at my surroundings.

The ceiling above me wasn't exactly a ceiling—it was made of canvas. The space wasn't large, and I understood immediately that we were in a tent. However, as I surveyed the rest of the room, I saw that it was far from a typical camping situation. The fact that the shelter was made of canvas was the only giveaway to the fact that it was a tent. If it hadn't been for that, I would have assumed we were in an apartment.

The ground below us was covered with a well-loved Persian rug, and the man from the night before was seated at a small bistro table, typing away on a laptop. There was a comfortable-looking love seat in the corner, and striped throw pillows sat happily on the cushions. The tent was tidy, and there were posters on the canvas walls from music and art shows.

I had been tucked into a bed that was a double-stacked mattress. It was covered in a lovely, albeit worn calico quilt. A gas-powered lamp decorated the corner table that was opposite the love seat, and the overall feel of the room could best be described as vintage cool. It certainly wasn't my idea of tent living. I was more confused than ever.

"I'm sure you're wondering where you are. I should introduce myself. My name is Zephyr. I found you on the sidewalk last night. You were pretty sick. When you passed out, I knew I couldn't leave you out there. Someone would have taken advantage of you for sure, so I carried you in here. You certainly don't weigh much." The man had seemed so intimidating the night before, yet he exuded warmth and gentleness in the light of day.

"I-I'm... Willow. Th-thank you," I stammered.

This man carried me here? Is this where he lives? Does that mean he's homeless? And I thought he wanted to kill me. My brain was muddled with confusion, and I still wasn't quite sure what to think about the situation. It was all too much for me to process.

"So, is there someone I can call for you?" Zephyr pulled an iPhone out of his pocket. "I'm sure you have folks who are wondering where you are."

"Tate. I need Tate." I closed my eyes and sighed with relief, realizing the man was going to help me.

"Here you go. Give him a call." Zephyr gave me his cell phone, and I dialed Tate's number with shaking hands. He picked up on the first ring.

"Hello," he said quickly, and I heard the tension in his voice.

"Tate, it's me. I'm safe. Please come and get me." My voice broke and I broke into a sob. As hard as I tried to get the words out, they wouldn't come.

"Here, Willow, let me tell him where you are." Zephyr took the phone from my hand, introduced himself, and told Tate what happened to me the night before. He also suggested that Tate take me to be checked out by a doctor immediately, since I didn't appear to be feeling very well. After giving him the address and some brief directions, he hung up and placed the phone on the bistro table. "He's on his way. Your man will be here to get you soon."

"Thank you so much for everything. I can't believe you carried me here and took care of me. You let me sleep in your bed. I don't know what would have happened to me if you hadn't taken it upon yourself to do that for me." I wiped the tears from my eyes and looked at the benevolent stranger.

"No problem, little lady. We're all human, after all. Isn't that what we're supposed to do? Look out for one another?" Zephyr smiled. I could tell he had a beautiful soul.

"Yes, it is what we should do. Unfortunately we don't

always do that. I appreciate your kindness more than you know."

"Kindness is what makes the world go 'round, Willow. That's a cool name, by the way," he replied.

"My mother was a hippie who grew up in a commune. Your name is pretty amazing, too." I grinned, feeling optimistic for the first time in days. "So, is this your home, Zephyr?"

"It is. It's a pretty comfortable pad, as far as that goes." He shrugged.

"I have to hand it to you. It doesn't look much like a tent at all. You've made it quite comfortable. But Zephyr... you're homeless," I stated the obvious.

"Technically, I suppose I am, but it doesn't feel that way to me. The people out here are my family. We look out for each other." He grinned.

Zephyr and I chatted some more while we waited for Tate to arrive. I found out that he was a student, working his way through college, and that he lived in the tent because he couldn't afford the outrageous cost of housing in Portland. He had no family, and no one to help him with tuition and living expenses. His only supporters were the people who lived on the streets alongside him. I'd never truly realized what a privileged life I'd lived until recently. Meeting Zephyr and finding Juniper had given me a whole new perspective on what was important.

"Willow," I heard Tate's frantic voice outside of the tent. "Willow, where are you?"

Forgetting my dizziness and nausea, I jumped up and ran to find him. When I saw his face, I began to sob as a million emotions bubbled to the surface. All the fear, pain, confusion, and desperation of the past few days swirled around inside of me as the tears streamed freely down my cheeks.

I grabbed Tate, flinging myself into his strong, protective arms. I never wanted to leave those arms again. I wanted to be married to those arms, and to be forever connected to the man who owned them. My hands shook as I traced my fingertips along his jawline. I never wanted to stop looking at him. I wanted the imprint of his face in my mind forever.

"Oh, babe, I've been going out of my mind with worry for you." Tate held me tightly and crushed his lips against mine with a kiss that I prayed would never end.

Like all good things, though, the kiss did end, and when we caught our breath, Tate wiped the tears from my face with his hands and looked at me closely. "The man who took you in said you were sick. What did he mean? What's wrong?"

"I don't know, Tate. I'm dizzy and nauseated. I passed out last night. I think it's probably just stress from everything that's been happening, but maybe he's right. Maybe I do need to see a doctor."

I was actually pretty worried about what was going on inside of my body. My mother had died of cancer at a very young age, and that fact was always in the back of my mind. *What if I have cancer, too?*

"The hospital is going to be our first stop." He reached down and scooped Omelet into his arms. "Thank you so much for taking care of her. You don't know how much that means to me." Tate smiled at Zephyr before leading me toward his car.

"Thank you again, Zephyr. I'm glad we were able to meet," I called to my new friend as we left.

"It was my pleasure, Willow. I'm glad you're back

where you're supposed to be. Maybe I'll see you around." He smiled widely and waved to us.

"I'm going to make a point of doing something nice for that man, Tate," I said as we got into the car.

"I'm sure you will. Let's just get you checked out first, babe," Tate said as he helped me fasten my seat belt.

"For once, I'm not going to argue with you. I have so much to tell you, but right now I'm just really glad you're here."

CHAPTER TWENTY

After dropping Omelet off at the apartment, Tate drove me straight to the emergency room, and I didn't even try to change his mind. Between the thump to the head that Diana had given me and the nagging feeling of general sickness, I knew I needed to be checked out.

Poor Tate always has to take care of me. I honestly don't know what the man sees in me. I'll be even harder to deal with if I'm really sick.

Mostly, though, I just prayed that my worst fears weren't confirmed. *What if I have cancer? What if I end up dying young, just like my mom did?* The horrible thoughts kept playing over and over again, like a broken record inside of my brain. I kept telling myself to stop thinking about it, but no matter how hard I tried, I kept coming back to the dreaded C-word.

What am I going to do if they tell me I'm dying? I'm not ready to die.

We pulled into the emergency room parking lot, and Tate led me inside of the crowded building. He knew the lady at the registration desk, and I think he must have pulled a few strings because we didn't have to wait long.

Within minutes I was seated on the hospital bed, and before I knew it, I was decked out in a stylish rear-end-exposing gown. The physician, Dr. Arroyo, arrived and asked Tate to step outside while he did the exam. Tate didn't look happy about leaving me, but he did as he was told.

Dr. Arroyo poked and prodded me, asked me about a million questions, and then did an invasive, full-body examination. After all that fun was over, he sent in the vampires to take a blood sample. The stinging, cold needle in my vein did nothing at all to help my queasiness, and I thought for sure that I was going to pass out again.

The doctor patted me on the shoulder and said he would let me know the results as soon as he could. When I asked him exactly what he was testing for, he just smiled and said it was routine lab work.

Routine lab work? I don't buy it. He asked me about my family medical history, and I told him about my mom. I just know they're screening me for cancer.

Unaware of my inner personal struggle, Dr. Arroyo said I should lie back and get comfortable, assuring me that he would talk with me when the tests came back.

He left the room and went into the hallway to let Tate know he was free to join me in the room again. Tate's face was a little more pale than usual, and I knew he was worried about me. "How are you feeling now? Any better?" He sat in the chair beside the hospital bed and held my hand.

I'm terrified that I'm dying, Tate. I'm going to end up just like my mother. I'm going to die and leave you all alone.

I swallowed hard, but I didn't say the words that were

swirling around inside of my head. Instead, I just started talking, hoping the terrible thoughts would eventually fade away.

"No, I'm not really feeling any better. It just seems like the room won't stop spinning, and I'm always on the verge of losing my lunch. It's not pleasant, to say the least. What do you think is wrong with me?"

"I don't know. Maybe it's stress. You've had a really tough few weeks, babe. You also told me you got knocked out."

"Yeah, I did. Do you think I have a brain injury?" I looked at him helplessly. *Or cancer?* I couldn't help but imagine the worst possible outcome.

"I doubt you have a brain injury, but it does sound like you got hit pretty hard," Tate replied thoughtfully.

"I was knocked out and kidnapped by a crazy woman! It was Diana Wilmington, do you remember her? Stepmother number two? Can you believe she came after me?" I was sure Tate would be surprised by my revelation, but I was shocked to see that he wasn't.

"Yep, she always was a piece of work. It looks like she hasn't changed much over the years." Tate nodded as he squeezed my hand. "I still don't understand why you were out wandering the streets alone in the middle of the night, Willow. Why didn't you and Diana come to meet us? Why didn't you stick to the plan?"

"What are you talking about? What plan? Do you mean to tell me you knew where I was all along?" My forehead wrinkled in confusion. *How does Tate know any of this?*

"Yes, of course I did. We all knew where you were. When your dad got the ransom note from Diana, he called me and Marcus right away. The three of us had a plan hatched within fifteen minutes. Your father told Diana that we would meet the two of you last night at eleven o'clock with the ransom money in hand. We wanted to wait until after dark so we could have police backup with us. We showed up at the designated spot, but you guys didn't. We had no idea where she was holding you, so we didn't know what to do. I was going out of my mind with worry until you called this morning. By the way, Marcus said he'll be over here soon to take your statement. They found Diana in her house, and hauled her off to jail. She was pretty groggy. It seems she took a couple of very potent sleeping pills. I don't suppose you know anything about that, do you? It doesn't matter. She's going to prison for a very long time." Tate rambled on as he stroked my hand lightly with his fingertips.

"Well, it seems like I blew that whole plan right out of the water," I said as I collapsed onto the pillow in disbelief. "I guess I jumped the gun and took matters into my own hands about an hour too soon. I asked Diana if she'd heard from Dad and she said no." I shook my head in frustration.

"She was obviously lying to you. I'm sorry you fell for it. You must have felt completely abandoned." Tate smoothed my hair away from my forehead. "Tell me what happened next."

"Well, when it seemed that my time was running out, I decided that Dad thought I wasn't worth five million dollars. So I figured that the only way out of the situation was to save myself. Not knowing what else to do, I cooked Diana some pasta primavera, drugged her food with sleeping pills, and took off on foot with Omelet. I had no idea where I was, and I couldn't find my bag, so I had no phone, and no money. I was really in quite a pickle, so all I could do was hoof it all the way from Vancouver to Portland. I was so sick and exhausted, and I finally passed out on the streets of Portland, where I was rescued by my new friend, Zephyr. I really like that guy, by the way. I think I'm going to offer him a job." I smiled at Tate, who leaned down and kissed me softly.

"You are one in a million, you know that, babe? I think we all underestimated your ability to take care of the situation yourself. But just know this: whatever happens, I will always come for you. You can count on it. Tattoo it on your arm, do whatever it takes so you don't forget it. I will *always* rescue you."

"I guess I know that, but sometimes a girl just has to rescue herself, Tate." I looked into his eyes and knew there was so much more I needed to tell him. The fear was still there, but the love I had for him was finally strong enough to overshadow it.

I took a deep breath and continued, "There's a lot I'm not sure about when it comes to marriage, Tate. I told you from the beginning that I had no idea how to be in love, and for the most part, that's still completely true. But over the last few days, I've started to understand something. I don't have to have all the answers. We can figure it out as we go. We can make our own perfectly imperfect relationship. One thing I know for sure is that we always manage to find our way back to each other. We were meant to be together, and I'm done questioning it."

My heart was racing, but I knew I had to say the words I should have said a long time ago. "I know I've been fickle and wishy-washy about getting married, but I'm ready now. I want to be your wife. I want to marry you. I'll marry you right now if you can figure out how to get someone in here to do it."

"For real, babe? You're really ready? You're not afraid

anymore?" The look on Tate's face melted my heart just a little bit more.

"Of course I'm afraid. I'm terrified! I don't think I'll ever *not* be afraid. I grew up watching my dad fall into one disastrous relationship after another, and I just feel like the odds of me being able to have a healthy marriage aren't very good. I'm not exactly what anyone would call 'wife material.' But I love you so much that it hurts, and I don't want any future unless you're in it. And it all became crystal clear to me while I was walking across the Interstate Bridge. Love is really all we need to make this work. It sounds sappy and cliché, but it's the truth. And I love you so much, Tate. So let's do it. Let's get married." Tears were streaming down my cheeks by that point, but I didn't care.

Just when I thought I had revealed it all, I remembered something horrible, and with a sinking heart, I realized that the revelation might change everything. I had never told Tate about that night with Marcus, and I knew I couldn't continue to keep the secret any longer. Lying and keeping things from him wasn't fair, and it wasn't right. If Tate and I were going to get married, we had to start the journey on the right foot.

"But there's one more thing, Tate. Since I'm baring my soul to you, I have to tell you everything. Before you jump into marriage with both feet, I need to tell you that I've been keeping something from you, something big. And once I tell you, I'm not sure if you're still going to want to marry me." I took a deep breath and told myself that I was doing the right thing. Tate deserved to know everything, even the things I'd rather keep hidden.

"There is absolutely nothing you can tell me that will make me not want to marry you." Tate smiled widely and squeezed my hand tightly.

"I wouldn't be too sure about that." I swallowed twice, trying to soothe the parched lining of my throat. "All right, here goes. A few weeks ago, the night that Marcus came over and watched that cat documentary with me, we fell asleep on my couch. *Together*. I woke up in his arms, Tate. Nothing happened, but I know how you feel about Marcus. So just go ahead and tell me that you don't want to marry me after all." I closed my eyes and braced myself for the impact.

Much to my surprise, Tate laughed out loud. "You're kidding, right? That's your big revelation? Do you mean to tell me you thought I didn't know about that?"

Tate's words caused my eyes to fly open.

"What do you mean you knew?" I couldn't believe what I was hearing. *How can he possibly know about what happened between me and Marcus?*

"Willow, Marcus called me that morning. He told me what happened, and he apologized profusely for falling asleep on your couch with you next to him. He also told me that you punched him in the face, and that gave me a pretty good laugh. Marcus and I worked everything out. He told me it wasn't a big deal, but that he wanted to be up-front with me. It meant a lot to me that he was so honest." Tate shrugged nonchalantly, as if my monumental secret was of absolutely no consequence.

"So let me get this straight. You're saying that you've known about this all along? I've been torturing myself with guilt for weeks, trying to figure out how to say the words, and you already knew?" I released the large breath I'd been holding inside. "Why didn't you say anything to me?"

"I didn't say anything because it didn't matter. It wasn't important to me. I trust you with my life, Willow. I know you would never be unfaithful to me. You would never intentionally hurt me, just like I would never hurt you. We love each other, and nothing else matters." Tate's mile-wide smile made my heart flip-flop in my chest.

"Tate—" I began, but my words were interrupted by a knock on the door.

"Miss Simpson, may I come in, please?" Dr. Arroyo called from the hallway.

"Of course. Come on in," I replied as I tried to compose myself. "Dr. Arroyo, this is my fiancé, Tate Randall."

"Hello, Doctor," Tate said as he extended his hand.

"It's nice to meet you, Mr. Randall." He shook Tate's hand.

My heart alternated between beating wildly inside of my chest and threatening to stop completely. *This is the moment of truth.* I clenched my hands into fists as I waited for Dr. Arroyo to speak. I just knew he was going to tell me that I had cancer. My life was a series of two steps forward and one step back.

"What's wrong with me, Dr. Arroyo? Why do I feel so horrible? Is it brain trauma? Or is it cancer?" I spoke the last word in nearly a whisper, having difficulty even saying it out loud. "Am I going to die like my mother did? Tell it to me straight. I can take it." My eyes filled with fresh tears, and I had to focus on my breathing because I felt like I was on the verge of hyperventilating.

"Miss Simpson, please calm down. You don't have a brain injury, and as far as I can tell, you don't have cancer. I know all about your mother's illness, but there's absolutely nothing to indicate that you're sick. A family history of cancer doesn't always mean you'll get it yourself. To the best of my knowledge, you're not going to die any time soon." He smiled kindly at me and scribbled some notes into his chart.

"I don't have cancer? Then what's wrong with me? I know the way I've been feeling is not normal." I squeezed Tate's hand tightly. *If it's not cancer, what could it be?*

"Dizziness and nausea are quite common during pregnancy, especially in the first trimester. So the good news is there's nothing wrong with you, other than the fact that your baby is doing a good job of making his or her presence known." Dr. Arroyo grinned at us, clearly enjoying our surprise.

"Ba-baby? I'm pregnant? That's... well, that's just... not possible," I stammered in confusion. "You must be mistaken."

"Are you sure, Dr. Arroyo?" Tate asked quietly.

"I'm absolutely sure, Mr. Randall. And it is entirely possible, Miss Simpson. Surely you don't need me to give you a biology lesson, do you?" The doctor chuckled.

"Well no, but... it's just... I can't... I don't know how...," I began, but I couldn't finish.

"I'll give you two a few minutes alone. I'm going to write you a prescription for a prenatal vitamin, and then I'll send in my nurse to answer all of your pregnancy questions. She's also going to give you a few referrals for obstetricians. Congratulations, you two." Dr. Arroyo nodded to us before leaving the room.

I took a deep breath and turned to look at Tate. His eyes glistened with tears, and a few escaped and ran down his cheeks. "A baby, Willow. We're going to have a baby." He gripped my hand tightly and brought it to his lips. I felt his hands tremble as he kissed my fingertips.

"Are you happy about it? You look happy."

The grin on Tate's face told me that he thought the news was great. I wasn't quite there yet. I was working hard to process all the emotions that were warring inside of me, but I knew that was going to take a very long time.

"Of course I'm happy. I'm ecstatic! All I've ever wanted was to be your husband and to have a family with you. But I think your feelings are a bit more complicated than mine, since having a child was never really on your agenda." He looked into my eyes, rose from the chair, and took a seat next to me on the hospital bed. "So I guess the real question is... are *you* happy, babe?"

"You know, Tate, I think it's way too soon for me to say whether or not I'm happy. I'm shocked, and I'm worried. Most of all, I'm terrified because I have no idea how to be a good mother. I can't even remember mine, and I honestly never, ever pictured myself as one. I'm a little bit afraid of babies. They're really scary. They remind me of wrinkly little raisins. All they do is eat, cry, and poop." I noticed that Tate's smile faded and his face fell a bit as I spoke.

I chose my next words carefully as I continued. "But I can tell you one thing, Tate Randall. This baby is a part of you, and there's not a single part of you that I don't love with all of my heart. So to answer your question, I would say that as soon as the shock wears off, I think the happiness is going to come."

By that point I was ugly crying, and trails of snot were running down my face. Tate grabbed a tissue and handed it to me. I gulped in too much air and managed to hiccup loudly. After I cleaned myself up and regained some control of my emotions, he gathered me into his arms and kissed me.

When the kiss ended, he continued to hold me closely, caressing my back in long, even strokes. "We're going to be parents. We're going to have a baby."

"It's crazy to think about, isn't it? I'm going to be someone's mom. You know what this means, right? It means that now we really need to get married," I replied quietly.

"You know I'm not going to argue about that one, babe. I've just been waiting for you to say when."

"I don't think an October wedding is going to work out, though."

"I know. You think it's too soon. That's all right."

"No, Tate. It's not soon enough. Having a baby changes everything. We need to do it now. Today, if we can." I smiled as the words slipped out of my mouth.

"Today? Are you trying to kill me? First I find out I'm going to be a father, and then you tell me that you want us to get married today. I'm not sure if my heart can take it." Tate's voice quivered with emotion.

"Well, I don't know what the law is, so I guess we need to do our research, but as soon as we can do it, let's go to the courthouse and get married. No more dragging my feet. I'm all in." My heart beat wildly inside my chest, but for the first time in a very long time, it wasn't out of fear.

"I'm going to look up Oregon marriage laws right now. I'm taking you up on it before you change your mind again," Tate teased with a grin.

"So I guess this means I'm going to have to be an adult after all. Also, I hope you know that the crazy pregnancy hormones are going to kick in and I'm going to be crying all the time. And when I'm not crying, I'm going to be driving you batty with my full range of emotional instability. I'm going to have insane cravings, and I'm going to grow out of all my clothes, and I just know I'll be a nightmare of a pregnant lady. Are you sure you're up for the challenge?" I looked at his face and smiled widely as the full impact of the news finally began to settle in.

"I have gladly taken on the challenge of loving you since

I was a little kid. I'm an old pro at it by now. No one can do it better than I can," he replied without even a second of hesitation.

It wasn't long before Dr. Arroyo told me I could go home. As much as I wanted to rest, there was something I needed to do first.

"Let's go to the courthouse, Tate. I want to get married," I said as we walked out of the hospital.

"Right now? Are you sure?"

"I've never been more certain of anything in my life," I replied.

Something happened to me the moment Dr. Arroyo said I was going to have a baby. All the fickle, unsettled thoughts and all-consuming fears about commitment seemed inconsequential in the light of finding out I that was going to be someone's mother. Not wanting to wait another second, we headed right to the courthouse, obtained our marriage license, and begged the county clerk to waive the typical three-day waiting period.

"In Multnomah County, we can only waive the waiting period for five extra dollars and a good cause," the clerk replied with a smile.

"I was kidnapped and held for five million dollars' ransom. I escaped and walked from Vancouver to Portland in the middle of the night. I was rescued by a homeless man named Zephyr after I passed out on the street," I explained.

"And we just found out that she's pregnant," Tate added with a proud smile.

"Well, if that doesn't qualify as a good cause, then I don't know what does. Have a seat and I'll see if I can convince Judge Fillmore to put it on his schedule," the clerk instructed.

"Do we have time to call her father?" Tate asked quickly.

"Yes, it may be a bit of a wait," she answered.

"You want to call my dad? Are you sure?" I asked Tate.

"I'm sure. He needs to be here," Tate said as he grabbed his phone to call him.

I was certain that he wouldn't come, but less than an hour later, my father walked through the door. I expected him to chastise me for both the Diana incident as well as our hasty marriage idea. Instead, he grabbed my hands, pulled me toward him, and hugged me tighter than he ever had in my life.

"I thought I'd lost you, Willow. Don't ever scare me like that again," he whispered in my ear, his voice cracking with emotion. "Now let's get this show on the road. Where is Judge Fillmore? He's an old golfing buddy of mine. I called him on the way over here and told him he would be marrying my daughter today."

"You did that? Thanks, Dad," I said as my eyes filled with tears.

"You're my only child. If I can't pull a few strings with a judge now and then, what's the point of being the richest man in Oregon? Besides, I would do anything for you."

Dad grabbed my hand as Judge Fillmore walked into the room. The two men exchanged niceties, and then the judge led us into his chambers. It was all happening so quickly, and I realized that I was about to become Tate's wife. Rather than feeling anxious, I knew I was exactly where I was supposed to be.

"Tate, do you take Willow to be your lawfully wedded wife, to have and to hold from this day forward, for better, for worse, for richer, for poorer, in sickness and health, until death do you part?"

"I do," he answered confidently.

Judge Fillmore turned toward me and recited the same wedding vows he'd just said to Tate. I'd heard the words hundreds of times before, but I had never given them much thought until that moment. As I listened, I realized that Tate and I had been doing these things for each other our whole lives. We'd been taking care of each other for as long as I could remember. Suddenly, all my fears seemed crazy, and I knew I wanted to be Tate's wife more than I had ever wanted anything.

When the judge asked for my answer, I said, "I do," without hesitation, closing my eyes as the tears began to fall once again. A sweet, long-forgotten memory floated to the surface of my mind.

Tate and I were ten years old, and we were on the playground at recess. We were sitting under the shade of a large tree so my ghostly white skin wouldn't get sunburned and blistered. From my spot on the sidelines, I watched as the other kids were playing.

Suddenly, I turned to Tate and asked, "What do you want to be when you grow up?"

Without missing a beat, he replied, "I want to be married to you."

I had laughed at him, punched him in the arm, and teased him. I told him that no one knew who they wanted to marry when they were ten years old.

In typical Tate fashion, he didn't argue with me. He didn't even try to convince me that he was right. Instead, he just smiled and said, "You'll see. I'm going to marry you. And someday you'll remember everything I said."

I finally understood that "someday" was here. Tate was right; I remembered every word he'd said that day. I thought about how lucky I was to be so completely loved by him. He had been devoted to me for as long as I could remember. He'd spent his life taking care of me, and he'd never wavered in his commitment. Tate had known at ten years old what it took me a lifetime to figure out—when love is right, nothing else matters.

FIVE MONTHS LATER

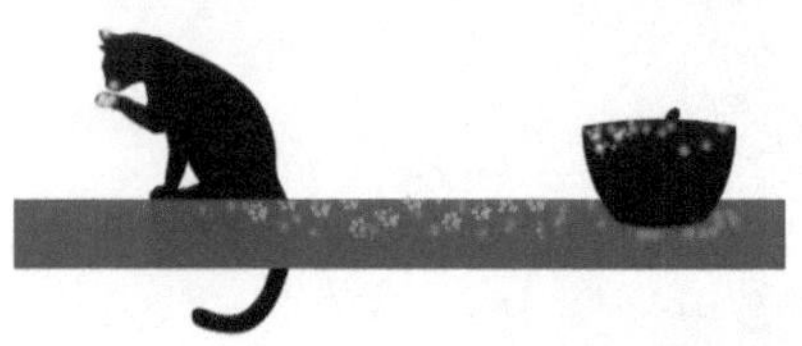

"Mrs. Randall, Dr. Stinson will see you now." Nurse Lori, my favorite OB nurse, poked her head into the waiting room and motioned for me to follow her down the hallway. "Mr. Randall, if you'll wait just a few minutes, we'll call you back when the doctor's ready."

I smiled, gave my husband a quick kiss on the cheek, grabbed my purse, and slowly rose to my feet.

"I'll see you in a few minutes, babe," Tate called as the door closed behind me.

"You're going to be in room three, Mrs. Randall, but we're going to make a quick stop at the scales first. Come right this way," Nurse Lori said.

As I walked behind her, I thought about how jarring it still was when I heard myself referred to as "Mrs. Randall." I kept thinking I would get used to it, but that hadn't happened yet. I had no idea how long it usually took a person to adjust to a new name, but I was still getting there. After all, I had been Willow Simpson my whole life; I had only been Willow Randall for a few months. I was still coming to terms with the fact that I was Tate's wife, and even though I had already felt the fluttery movements inside of me, the idea that I was going to be a mother continued to surprise me.

Nurse Lori gestured for me to step onto the scale, and she checked my weight. She wrote the number in my chart, and I was pretty sure I saw her raise her eyebrow in surprise.

I gulped when I saw the number. *Is this scale wrong? It has to be wrong. There's no way I've already gained more than thirty pounds!*

When we were finished, we went into room three and she told me to take a seat, then checked my blood pressure and temperature, noting that both were just fine and well within the normal ranges. When the preliminary exam was completed, Nurse Lori told me to take off my clothes and put on the gown she handed me. Once she left the room, I did as I was instructed.

Prompt, as usual, it wasn't long before Dr. Stinson, my obstetrician, came into the room. "Well, Willow, are you ready? It's the big moment. You get to see your baby today." She grabbed my hand to help me onto the examination table in her office.

My clumsy, unwieldy body was its usual uncooperative self. Pregnancy had caused my awkwardness to skyrocket to a whole new level. The state of being pregnant was like an all-too-real version of *Invasion of the Body Snatchers*.

"I guess I'm as ready as I'll ever be," I replied as I plopped down unceremoniously.

"So we're going to do your ultrasound today. Have you decided whether or not you want to know the sex of your baby?" Dr. Stinson tilted her head to the side as she asked.

"Well, Tate and I have been going back and forth for

weeks, trying to decide if we wanted to know or if we wanted to be surprised. We were able to make a good argument for both cases, but late last night we finally agreed that we want to know." I squirmed on the table, trying to get comfortable. When I finally managed it, I sighed and rested my head on the flat pillow.

"All right then. Hopefully the little one cooperates and gives us a good view. We're usually able to get a pretty accurate visual image with our regular ultrasound at around twenty weeks, but I also have the new three- and four-dimensional ultrasound equipment, so you'll get an even clearer picture. We'll hope for good results." She smiled.

Dr. Stinson was an amazing doctor. She was actually one of my regular customers at the Dancing Crêpe, and I'd been surprised when I found her name on the list of obstetrics referrals from Dr. Arroyo. We already knew each other, so I felt comfortable with her from the very beginning. She had endless amounts of patience for my crazy, never-ending prenatal questions, and she never made me feel stupid for asking them.

So far, my pregnancy seemed to be progressing normally. The first half of it had been pretty uneventful, other than the fact that I was already as big as a house and I had to buy a whole new wardrobe. I was hoping the second half would go smoothly, and that the weight gain and weird food cravings would start to slow down.

"How have you been doing? Is the nausea any better than last month?" she asked.

"I suppose I'm doing all right, even though I seem to be riding a continuously looping emotional roller coaster. I'm glad that at least I've been feeling better than I was. The dizziness and nausea seem to have finally passed, thank goodness, but I absolutely cannot stand the smell of bacon.

What's up with that? It's the strangest thing, because normally I love bacon. I mean, who doesn't love bacon? Apparently me. Anyway, it makes cooking a little bit difficult, that's for sure. I've actually taken to wearing nose plugs at work, and that seems to help a little bit," I babbled on with a roll of my eyes.

Dr. Stinson just nodded, as if it were all par for the course. "Hopefully that will pass soon as well. Your weight is all right, although I do have to say that you've gained a bit more than I would have assumed at this point. It's probably all those crêpes that you eat, right? I know I can't seem to get enough of them." She grinned and scribbled some notes into my chart.

"I'm a little bit surprised that I've gained so much weight already, although I probably shouldn't be. I mean, let's be honest. I'm starving all the time. It feels like I can't consume enough food. I'm always dreaming of my next meal, even while I'm eating the current one. If things don't change, I'll look like a beached whale before it's all over," I replied with a sigh and a shake of my head.

"Hmmm... well, we'll keep an eye on that for sure," she said as she scribbled something else into the chart.

My weight had never been an issue before I had become pregnant. I'd always been on the skinny side, and no matter what I did, I never gained weight. Needless to say, I'd been a bit taken aback when I stepped on the scale earlier. I knew I'd turned into a one-woman eating machine, but the fact that I'd already gained over thirty pounds was ridiculous. I was only halfway through the pregnancy! I was going to have to try to rein in my appetite. That wasn't going to be easy, though, considering food was my life.

"So, Nurse Lori says you have quite a crowd in the waiting room, Willow. Do you want them all to be in the room with you while we do the ultrasound?" The doctor turned on the monitor and rummaged through her drawer for her gloves.

The whole gang had insisted upon coming to the appointment. I wasn't even sure if they would be allowed into the room, but I'd told them to come along anyway. Dad, Marcus, Elizabeth, Cinnamon, Nellie, Wyatt, Suzanne, and Juniper were all there. Juniper had even hidden Omelet away inside of her bag, and I was pretty sure Dr. Stinson wouldn't be pleased if she found out. It hadn't felt right to leave Omelet out of such a momentous occasion, though. I didn't want her to feel neglected. She was going to have to share the attention before too long, and I wanted her to know that I loved her just as much as I always had.

"Yeah, I've brought along the whole motley crew. Sorry about that. I was hoping it could just be me and Tate at first, and once we know the sex, maybe everyone else can come in and see the picture?" I had no idea if that was the usual protocol, but I had a feeling that Dr. Stinson would accommodate me if she was able to do so.

"Well, normally that's not how it works, but you're my favorite chef. And you're also my last patient for the day, so I think we can make it happen." She smiled. "I'll go call Tate in now, and we'll get started."

The nervous feeling of butterflies flapping around in my ever-growing abdomen was a bit unsettling. I'd been simultaneously anticipating and dreading my first ultrasound since the moment I learned I was pregnant. I was curious and excited to see my little one floating around inside of me, but I was also afraid. What if something was wrong? What if Dr. Stinson found some sort of complication? What would I do then?

I was amazed at how quickly I'd become attached to the

little human growing in my uterus. It had taken me a few weeks to really get used to the idea of a baby, but once I did, I was hooked. Knowing there was a life inside of me, a life that had been created out of the love Tate and I shared for each other, had proven to be the most eye-opening, earth-shattering thing I'd ever experienced. I had never been so happy and content, and I didn't want anything to steal that joy from me.

"Hey, babe. Are you ready to see our little one?" Tate came through the door and sat on the chair beside the table.

"I think I am. I also think that I might pass out from the stress and anxiety, so either way, it'll be an eventful experience." I smiled and grabbed his hand.

"I learned a long time ago that everything is an eventful experience with you. But I like it that way," Tate replied with a shrug and a wink.

"All right, you two, let's get started. Willow, I'm going to squirt some of this gel on your belly. I've tried to warm it up a bit, but it still might feel a little cold and strange. After that, I'm going to slide my Doppler around and try to find a clear picture of your little one. It's not going to hurt at all, so don't worry about anything. The image can be a bit confusing to understand at first, but I'll point out all the important parts once we get the shot. Are you ready?" Dr. Stinson smiled.

"I'm as ready as I'll ever be," I told her.

Please don't let anything be wrong. I don't think I can handle it.

I flinched a little as she squirted the slimy gel onto my belly, then watched the screen in anticipation. Several blurry images moved across the monitor, but I had a hard time deciphering any of it. It all looked like one confusing, muddled, giant blob to my untrained eyes.

Is that what my baby looks like?

"Oh my. How did I miss this?" Dr. Stinson whispered under her breath. "Well, that's unexpected."

"Unexpected? What's wrong, Dr. Stinson?" Tate leaned forward in his seat, his eyes widening in fear.

"Please tell me there's nothing wrong with my baby," I said breathlessly as I gripped Tate's hand so hard that I nearly broke the bones.

"Well... nothing's wrong. Please don't panic. It's just that... well...." Dr. Stinson's eyes met mine, and the smile on her face began to spread. "It looks like you doubled your recipe, chef."

"I'm sorry, what? Doubled my recipe? What do you mean?" I shook my head in confusion.

"Willow, Tate, you're having twins. Congratulations!" She stopped moving the Doppler on my abdomen and pointed to the screen. "Look, you can see them right there. There are two heartbeats. That means you're having two babies. One is sort of hiding behind the other, but I managed to get a pretty good look at your little ones. And not only are you having twins, but you're going to get one of each—a boy and a girl."

"Twins? Are you kidding me?" I collapsed onto the pillow and blew out the giant breath I'd been holding. "No wonder I'm as big as a house! There are two human beings inside of me."

"This is amazing news. I can't quite believe it." Tate grinned widely and wiped tears from his eyes. "We're having twins, babe."

"Just hold up a minute. Are you sure, Dr. Stinson?" It wasn't that I didn't believe her; it was just all so unexpected.

"I'm absolutely sure. I don't know how I missed it before, but at all your other checkups, I've only ever detected one heartbeat with my stethoscope. That happens sometimes with twins, especially when they're positioned like yours are, with one hiding behind the other. I suppose this is another good reason that we do an ultrasound around this time. It gives us a much clearer picture of what's going on inside. Look at the screen. It's all right there." She gestured toward the ultrasound monitor.

Staring in wonder at the picture of the two heartbeats of my children, my cheeks grew damp as the tears coursed down them. I felt as if I'd just been handed the entire world on a silver platter. How was it possible that I'd never known this was perfectly, exactly, everything I wanted?

"It's pretty unbelievable, isn't it?" Tate said with a twinkle in his eyes. "Twins. I know just what we should name them, too."

"Name them? You mean you've made it that far already? I'm still reeling from the shock. I'm sitting here trying to figure out where we're going to put two babies in our tiny apartment, and I'm also trying to calculate how many diapers two babies will go through in a week. When am I supposed to sleep? Will I ever get to take a shower? How will I go to work with two infants? And how am I supposed to breastfeed two babies at the same time? I'm going to be like a milking cow." My brain was trying hard to keep up as the questions came flying one after another.

"I recommend that you just try to enjoy the moment, Willow. I know this is overwhelming news, but you don't have to figure it all out in the next twenty seconds." Dr. Stinson patted my hand comfortingly.

"You're right, I guess." I turned toward Tate and asked, "Okay, what should we name them?"

"We should name them after your mother," he answered proudly.

"After my mother? Well, I'm all for being progressive, Tate, but I don't think our son is going to appreciate being named Fern," I replied, my forehead wrinkled in confusion.

"Your mother's name was Fern Wolf Tremaine. We're getting one of each, so I say we name the girl Fern and the boy Wolf. What do you think?"

"Wow. I think you're the sweetest man in the world, and a genius. I sure hope our kids take after you. Fern and Wolf... yes, it's perfect, Tate," I agreed with a nod.

"I come up with some good things every once in a while." He grinned.

I stretched out my arm and rested one sweaty palm over my babies' heartbeats, the other on my abdomen. Tate set his hand on top of mine. Looking at the steady rhythm of my babies' hearts, I knew everything was going to be all right.

"Hello, Fern and Wolf. I'm your mom. And this hot firefighter right here? Believe it or not, that's your dad. I'm sure you're wondering how a girl like me landed a man like him. I know I wonder every single day. All I can say is I'm one lucky woman. You're going to figure out really soon how wonderful he is. He's going to be the best dad in the world. He always does everything right, and he has a knack for being perfect. Me, on the other hand? Well, I'm going to apologize up front for everything I'm going to do wrong. I'll let you in on a little secret—I have no idea how to be your mom. But I already love you more than I thought was possible, and I'm never going to stop trying to be the mom you deserve. I'll do my best to make all the right choices, but I know I'm going to fail. There's a lot I don't know, but I know how to love you. And I think I can learn the other things. If you can forgive me all the rest, then we're going to get along just fine."

I turned toward Tate and sighed. "Two babies? How am I possibly going to take care of two babies? I was worried that I couldn't even take care of one."

I looked from Tate to Dr. Stinson, hoping one of them would have some insightful words of wisdom. As usual, it turned out that my perfect husband knew just what to say.

"Together. That's how we're going to do it. Just like we do everything else." Tate hugged me tightly. "Should we call in the crew and tell them the news?"

"Oh yeah, I forgot they were all out there. They're going to freak out!" I smiled.

"I'll go get them," Dr. Stinson said.

Less than a minute later, the small room was filled with the expectant faces of our friends and family. I realized again how lucky I was to have so many people in my corner. With the news I'd just heard, I was going to need all the help I could get.

"So, don't keep us waiting any longer, Willow," Juniper said. I noticed her large bag was moving slightly, and I smiled knowing Omelet was inside.

"Yeah, what's the news, boss? It better be good since we closed the food truck for this." Wyatt grinned.

"I told you, Wyatt, she's having a boy. I just know it," Suzanne answered.

I noticed that his hand was clasped tightly inside of hers. When I introduced the two of them a few months ago, I had no idea that they would become so completely absorbed in one another. It made me glad to see that two of my closest friends had found happiness together. They really were a perfect pair.

"Don't keep us in suspense any longer. What's up with the ultrasound? What did you find out?" Marcus chimed in.

"It's a girl. And just so you know, Cinnamon and I have

already decided that we're in charge of her wardrobe. No offense, but you don't have an ounce of fashion sense, Willow, so we'll be taking over in that area," Elizabeth said with a smirk and a flip of her glossy blonde hair. Cinnamon nodded in agreement.

"No, it's a boy. Tate and I are going to teach him to play basketball," Marcus argued as he draped his arm across Cinnamon's shoulders.

"I can't believe I'm going to be a grandfather. Do I even look old enough to be someone's grandfather?" Dad checked his reflection in the mirror over the sink.

"So who's right, dear? Is it a boy or is it a girl?" Nellie asked as she stood next to me and squeezed my hand.

"Well, you're actually all correct. It's a boy...," I said.

"And a girl," Tate added.

"We're having twins," I explained.

"Oh my. I definitely don't look old enough to be the grandfather of twins." Dad smiled and shook his head in mock dismay.

"Twins? Oh my goodness. Well, I suppose it's not that hard to believe. Did you know your grandmother was a twin, Willow? And her mother was one also. It runs in our family," Juniper revealed.

"How is it possible that I didn't know that? I guess it explains a lot."

"Now you'll have to come up with two names," Cinnamon chimed in.

"Tate's already taken care of that. We're going to name them Fern and Wolf...," I started.

"After your mother," Dad finished, and his voice shook with emotion.

I noticed that Elizabeth grabbed his hand and held it tightly. My stepmother and I had our share of problems, but

I knew she really did love my father. After so many bad marriages, I was glad that he'd finally found his own happy ending, even if it had been a rocky beginning.

"Yes, Dad, we're naming them after Mom. We wanted to include her in some way, and Tate came up with the perfect plan. I think she would approve," I said as I met his gaze.

"She certainly would," he agreed.

He walked across the room, leaned down, and kissed me lightly on the top of the head. Dad was a man of few words, and even fewer feelings. He liked to keep his emotions hidden, but I was certain that I detected a few tears in his eyes as he turned and resumed his place beside his wife.

As everyone in the room began to talk at once and argue over who was going to get to babysit the twins first, Tate's eyes met mine and we smiled, sharing a look that didn't require words. It really felt as if we'd finally come full circle, and our story was continuing in exactly the way it should.

Dr. Stinson had said that I just doubled the recipe, and although she'd meant it as a joke, it was a pretty accurate description. As a chef, I knew that doubling any recipe had the potential to end in disaster. Oftentimes, bakers would avoid it altogether. Straying from the original directions could lead to having to adjust the cooking temperatures or ingredients in order to achieve an optimal final product. In theory, doubling a recipe shouldn't be a problem, but in baking, as in life, making changes widened the margin for error.

I guess I'd always been a bit of a gambler, though, because I doubled my recipes all the time. Maybe it was luck, or maybe it was skill, but it always worked out in the end.

Even though Tate and I had strayed from the original

directions, and even though the possibility for disaster was very real, we had doubled the recipe. And somehow I knew what I was baking would be the sweetest things I had ever created.

THE END

HUNKA HUNKA BURNIN' LOVE

(CHEF KIM OF CLASS COOKING'S
VERSION OF CREPE SUZETTE)

Crepes (makes 12):

1 cup flour
  ¼ teaspoon salt
  2 tablespoons sugar
  2 eggs
  1 cup milk
  ¼ cup water
  2 tablespoons orange liqueur (like Cointreau or Grand
Marnier)
  2 tablespoons butter melted

Whisk wet ingredients except butter together, then whisk in dry ingredients until smooth. Whisk in melted butter and refrigerate for at least 1 hour or overnight.

Cook the crepes in a preheated crepe pan with more butter as needed. Make small crepes- 6"to 8". Set cooked crepes on a plate with waxless paper in between each crepe.

Continue cooking crepes until all the batter is used. You should have 12 crepes.

Flambé Mixture and Sauce:

¼ cup orange liqueur
    ¼ cup brandy
    8 tablespoons butter
    ½ cup sugar
    zest of 1 orange
    zest of 1 lemon
    1 cup orange juice

Mix alcohol together in a measuring cup.

In 2 large sauté pans (or you can make 2 batches in the same pan), melt half of the butter, add half of each of the sugar, orange and lemon zests, and add half of the orange juice. When the mixture is bubbly and slightly caramelized remove from heat. Add crepes one at a time. Coat one side of the crepe with sauce. Then while still in the pan fold the crepe in half, and then fold in half again, making a triangle.

Push that triangle to one side of the pan, add another crepe, and continue the process until you have 6 folded crepes in the pan. Cover the bottom of the pan evenly with the crepe triangles. Place pan back onto the heat and bring to a boil, shaking the pan to distribute the sauce evenly over the crepes. Remove pan from the heat again and tip the pan to one side. Add half the brandy and liqueur (away from the heat). Return pan to the heat and ignite alcohol by tipping the pan toward the gas burner flame or lighting the alcohol with a match. Flambé shaking the pan gently until the flames subside and the alcohol is cooked off. Remove crepes and sauce from pan and keep them warm. Repeat for the next 6 crepes.

Serve warm with vanilla ice cream. Use 2 crepes per serving.

Serves 6.

ABOUT THE AUTHOR

Thanks for reading *JUST DOUBLE THE RECIPE*. I do hope you enjoyed Willow's continuing story. I appreciate your help in spreading the word, including telling a friend. Before you go, it would mean so much to me if you would take a few minutes to write a review and share how you feel so others may find my work. Reviews really do help readers find books. Please leave a review on your favorite book site.

Don't miss out on New Releases, Exclusive Giveaways and much more!

Join my newsletter: http://eepurl.com/cfhMXf
Join Heidi's Tribe (my reader group)
Follow my Blog: www.heidireneemason.wordpress.com
Visit my website for my current booklist:
www.heidireneemason.com

I'd love to hear from you directly, too. Please feel free to e-mail me at heidisbooks999@gmail.com or check out my website www.heidireneemason.com for updates.

ACKNOWLEDGMENTS

I would like to acknowledge the amazing staff at Hot Tree Publishing. Thank you all for being such a wonderful publishing family. I would also like to acknowledge my fantastic family and friends for always being there and supporting my crazy dreams.

www.ingramcontent.com/pod-product-compliance
Lightning Source LLC
Chambersburg PA
CBHW050533190726
48284CB00003B/1052